No Easier Road

No Easier Road

By
E. Okolo

Fourth Dimension Publishing Co., Ltd.

First Published 1985 by
FOURTH DIMENSION PUBLISHING CO., LTD
16 Fifth Avenue, City Layout. PMB. 01164, Enugu, Nigeria.
Tel+234-42-459969. Fax+234-42-456904.
email: fdpbooks@aol.com, fdpbooks@yahoo.com
Web site: http://www.fdpbooks.com.

Reprinted 2002

ISBN 978-156-156-4

CONDITIONS OF SALE

Design and Typesetting by
Fourth Dimension Publishers, Enugu

I

A

The day had been a lousy, irritating one with the temperature soaring to the middle-eighties in Fahrenheit. Twentieth June — one of the hottest days in a very hot month. Then suddenly, with that exciting pregnancy of nature, the weather had changed — clouds darkened, rain came down in torrential sheets and the clap of thunder was enough to scare spooks silly.

That was how it all started; on a lousy note. Benin City was beginning to glitter with sky scrapers and evil — the stink of day-light robberies and movie-like holdups was beginning to be smelt in place of the evil that was human sacrifice. Where the rich looked at the poor with disdain and the thrill of oil had put blights on peoples' eyes. Where it was common for beggars and unfortunates alike to watch in helplessness as the fortunates dipped their hands in oil and tasted of the powerful liquid.

She stood under a small shelter, watching the road with alert eyes as liquid rain thundered on the roof and thunder rumbled with a liquid voice. Her name was Ify. Ify Madu. She was born in a gutter and bred in the streets. Her mother was a mad woman who used to sit by the road-side during the day time, with a vacant stare while people dropped alms on her. And at night she slept in a dry gutter.

One certain day way back she was sitting by the road side, flies buzzing around her when Ify's father saw her. Ify's father had been a truck-pusher who toiled through rain and sunshine to scratch a living. On that day, he was pushing a truck when he set eyes on her sitting by the roadside. He stood there for some time staring at her, feeling something strange come over him. Then life stirred in his loins and his blood began to throb. Her sheer beauty which couldn't be hidden by the dirt and dust that had accumulated on her during all these years got to him badly.

Night found him creeping into the gutter where he met her sleeping. She wasn't wearing anything then and the sight of her naked beauty overwhelmed him. Whereas he had planned to rape her hard, the gentle side of him took over that night. He was gentle, loving and sympathetic as he disvirginized her. It hurt him a lot watching the blood seeping out and the pain in her eyes as he thrust deeper. He had returned the next day at the same time and taken her again. But this time he had seen a glint of pleasure in her mad eyes. For two months there after he usually came here to satisfy his desires and she was always waiting for him. Then one day he had been run over by a trailer. When she waited for him and he didn't come she had gone more berserk than before.

When Ify was born her mother had abandoned her in that gutter and fled to another location. The baby was found by a sane woman who also lived in the streets. She brought Ify up and sent her to beg for alms from the age of three. At ten she had run out on the woman to live with a wealthy household known as 'the Blems' as a house-girl. She lived there for seven years and grew to be a beautiful young woman, so beautiful that the respectable Mr. Blem took the risk of making love to her once a day and when his wife caught them, Ify was once again in the streets. To survive, Ify took to prostitution. And while in this trade she had met Joe Puna. From that moment unfortunate Ify was no longer helpless.

Lightning streaked across the sky and the growl of thunder followed in its wake. Ify glanced at her cheap wrist-watch. It read 5 pm. The man should be along anytime from now. Jimoh had said the man usually left his place of work at five. She looked up and down the deserted street with a little anxiety, hoping that there was no one somewhere who was watching her. Her heart was beating slightly faster than usual and as she transferred her handbag to her left hand, she noticed that her hands were shaking.

Suddenly she remembered Jimoh's flat voice and the deadly

menace in his eyes when he had assigned the job to her. He had ended the briefing with, "I don't have to remind you that this job's got to be handled right. Handle your part right and leave the rest to us. But botch the operation and I'll ....." "He had left the sentence hanging, but what she saw in his eyes was enough. It had made her flinch and even now she shivered involuntarily. Gilt Jimoh had never spoken to her this way. If her instincts were right this job was a prelude to something greater.

Smart Gilt. She had always known he was a smart guy. Trust Gilt to choose a deserted spot like this. Only two cars had passed since she started the watch and her legs were already beginning to hurt. Even the rain was not about to let up and she wasn't too sure if Gilt hadn't arranged for the rain. He could go to any length to ensure that his plans worked even if it meant arranging with heaven to open its bowels.

He had said it was going to be a white Range Rover and had made her memorize the plate number.

Yeah! The ideal place. The ideal time. And under ideal conditions! Trust Gilt. . . . .

"Botch it and I'll . . . ."

Then she saw the white Range Rover cruising at a moderate speed and her heart began to beat violently against its pericardial sac.

* *

Tim Aina was the proprietor of Omoregie Enterprises. A quiet man of around five feet six, and married with three kids. He was dark in complexion, with a face that had grown soft and harmless and a belly which was a pointer to the countless barrels of beer he had soaked over the years. Two days ago a party was held in his house to celebrate his forty-seventh birthday.

Aina jammed the accelerator to the floor-boards and felt the Rover lurch forward with a burst of speed that pleased him. Rain splashed and pattered on the windscreen and ran down in rivulets. He glanced at the briefcase beside him to make sure it was still there. Every Thursday of the week he usually went to collect Four Thousand naira from his bank so that the workers in Omoregie

Enterprises could be paid on Friday. So today, another Thursday, the briefcase contained Four Thousand in crisp naira bills.

The Rover plunged into large pot-hole, shuddered and emerged, the steering wheel shaking violently. At that speed, another car would have careened into the bush at the road-side but not the Range-Rover. Aina managed to bring it under control and relaxed speed, using a piece of cloth to wipe off the fog that was beginning to blur the windscreen. Then he saw someone ahead, standing in the rain and flagging him down desperately. He didn't like this place. It was very deserted for his taste. But the guy in the rain was soaking wet.

He slowed down and stopped a little ahead of the figure, wound down a side window and peered out. A girl! He had to help her. Most girls were naturally harmless. As she drew abreast with the car, Aina opened the right hand door and the girl clambered in. He engaged gear and the Rover moved off again. Glancing at her he saw that she was extremely beautiful. She was compact, four inches past the five feet line with raven black hair. Her legs were nice, without blemishes and the texture of her skin lighter than that of a full-blooded African. She had a small straight nose, a generous mouth that was matched by her dimpled cheeks and the finely shaped head. But it was her eyes that frightened him.

The brownish eyes had something hard about them, something he couldn't define. Noticing that he was peering at her eyes with a worried frown, she looked away hurriedly.

"Where are you going to?" He asked her.

"Anywhere, you can drop me where you please." There was a quaver in her voice.

"How come rain met you on such a lonely spot? If I hadn't come along you would still be there now."

"Had nothing to do. So I was wandering."

"Wandering?" His voice was incredulous. "What on earth should a' pretty girl like you be wandering for? You haven't a home or something?"

Ify felt a muscle in her temple twitch. She glared at him angrily. "Look mister, you're giving me a ride, not interrogating me. How can you suggest I don't have a home?"

Aina was immediately repentant. He was going too far. You tend to hurt people when you suggest they don't have homes. If he was going to get from her what he wanted this was no way to set about it. He glanced at her, scanning the throbbing of her blouse with his eyes. She really was desirable. He wanted her. His wife didn't have to know about this.

"Okay sis, I am sorry about this." He said in a chastened tone. "My name's Aina. Yours?"

"Mary Bolum." She said the first names that came to her mind. "You returning from work?"

"Yes." He said eagerly. He was glad that she had gotten over the insult. On further thought he added, "what do you do for a living if I may ask?"

"A bit of modelling here and there."

He glanced sideways at her, frowned and bit his lower lip, a trifle puzzled. He was sure that she had lied. The look in her eyes didn't belong to the modelling profession though he couldn't place where it belonged. If only she would meet his eyes.

Ify shivered convulsively. Her body was very cold and her hands shaky. It wasn't only the cold. The job ahead made her nervous and jittery. She had handled many jobs before but this was the first time she was going to stick a gun in a guy's face. Joe had taught her how to use the gun but this fleeting thought gave her no reassurance. Her instinct told her she was going to witness a horrible thing. All along, the gang had operated without her sticking a gun in someone's face but it seemed the *status quo* was changing.

"Your hands are shaking." Aina commented, a nervous note in his voice. The look in her eyes chilled him.

"This cold is unbearable. I've been standing in the rain for some time."

Instantly Aina relaxed. He knew how to handle cold women. His right hand went to her lap and felt the warmth there. Then the hand began tracing a gradual upward pattern, moving under her clothes with exploratory caution. She shuddered but didn't push him away. It was all part of the bait.

He leered at her wolfishly. Not able to control himself any longer his foot shifted from the accelerator to the brake then he grabbed her. She allowed him a moment's kiss then pushed him away firmly.

"Not here." She said, still not looking at him. "Let's reach the next junction first where there could be help if you want to rape me." Her mouth creased in a forced smile.

Aina shrugged, released the brake and trod on the gas again. Then she saw the next junction about two poles ahead and hurriedly opened her handbag. Her eyes and the harsh line that suddenly appeared on her mouth betrayed her. He swore softly, his hand shooting out immediately to grab her. But she shoved him violently with her left hand and before the twinkle of an eye a shiny automatic had appeared in her hand.

The Rover veered, entered a pot hole but he steered it back quickly to the road.

"Okay mister, take over your wheel. Stop at the next junction. Make a mistake and I'll spread your guts inside the Rover. Get moving!" She had the gun by her side so that in order to reach it the man had to pass her first.

Aina felt sick inside. She scared him silly. Well, he might have known, he thought. A gangster's moll. He didn't want her to see that he was scared. He had to play this bold.

"Look sister," he said in his most cajoling voice, "put that toy away." He softened his voice and even forced a grin. "Okay it's a joke. My broads play jokes on me sometimes." A shrug. "But I can't drive when a toy's stuck in my face."

"That junction. Go on! Drive! I won't tell you again. A word and you'll be in hell before you know it. And don't try any tricks. I have handled more than your match before."

Aina stared at her, licked his dry lips then grabbed the wheel. He told himself that he wouldn't try to cheat his wife after this if he got out of this jam. The Rover once more was in motion.

Inside, Ify's triumph had made her forget her earlier worries. She was exuberant. Joe should have seen me handle this. I bet he couldn't have handled it better. She even found it hard to believe that she had done this job. She remembered the briefcase.

"A nice briefcase you've got here." She said with ugly sarcasm. "How much have you got inside?"

"Four grand. What's it to you?"

She grinned. "You guys sure get along. I didn't know there was all this much money in the world."

"Stop it!" He shouted at her. She was irritating him with her sarcasm.

She placed her left hand on the briefcase. "You wouldn't be needing this. Four thousand is nothing to you. Even if you need it you wouldn't miss it. There are guys who don't see ten kobo in a day. They sure could do with this pile."

"Okay, stop here!" She commanded, jabbing the gun on to the back of Aina's neck.

Aina brought the Rover to a halt, his neck stiffening as the gun dug deeper. Instantaneously two men rushed out from a shrub nearby, opened the door on Aina's side.

"Come out mister!" Joe Puna hissed, his eyes glinting. He had a .38 automatic in his hand.

Aina stepped out meekly, followed by Ify who had the briefcase in her hand.

"Check whether the money is there." Aina instructed her. She checked, nodded and handed her gun to Joe. He came forward menacingly, jabbed the .38 into Aina's guts and frisked him quickly. "Okay, the bush there. And be snappy about it."

Aina wobbled over to the bush, his eyes scared. He didn't like the mean look on Joe's face. This guy was capable of murder without batting an eyelid.

"Lie down and bury your face in the ground."

Aina obeyed, his heart beating sluggishly. Then suddenly he glanced up to find Joe levelling the automatic on his skull.

"Oh please. No." He whimpered. "Give me a break I promise to bring more money for you if you want. Don't kill me please. I've got a pregnant wife and three kids."

Joe laughed horribly. His eyes were glinting with unsurpressed excitement. "So long mister."

The gun barked. A slug tore into the base of Aina's skull. Blood and brains flew about. He rose to his feet madly as death swept over him and began to run. He ran for a few steps when a gun banged again and tossed him into the air.

B

Dupe Aina walked over to the clock on the mantlepiece and checked the time for the umpteenth time. 8.00. Tim should have been back by now, she told hereself. She couldn't really place her hands on what was delaying him though she had a hunch. When your man starts coming home late from work everyday it could mean only one thing, trouble. And there had been plenty of it since this working week began. She had the feeling that he was beginning to go out with other women, precisely younger frills. Most women have that instinct. But she credited herself with more instincts than most women. If her 'superb' instincts were correct then her seventeen years of happy marriage to Tim was heading for the rocks.

All along their marriage had been a highly successful one — more successful than some of her friends'. It had been a source of immense pride to her .... that was before this working week set in. Come Monday and everything had changed. He would come back from work, feeling vibrant but with a smouldering temper that wasn't a part of his nature. He would curse, snarl and swear and even threaten. Dupe had told herself many times that this strange behaviour was a smokescreen to hide his guilt for something he had done. And this something she could guess though she couldn't be sure. The thing that infuriated her most was that all this while he wouldn't meet her eyes: Whenever she asked him what was wrong, he would snap at her while his eyes turned swiftly. Worse still he wouldn't confide in her as he used to. He had probably got bored with her and found himself a younger lover. This thought always turned her cold and made her recoil with jealousy. And this after all her faithfulness to him these seventeen years past.

But there existed a little doubt in her mind as to what was

keeping her husband so late this particular evening. And this doubt was blooming more by the minute. She was convinced that Tim wouldn't stay this long even if a dirty lover was in his arms. Could he have taken on a whore and she had got him into big trouble? The mere thought made her shudder. Then with steely determination she decided to phone the police if she tried his office again and there was no reply.

Dupe was a grossly fat woman with eyes like slits on her fat head. Thin lipped and with a sharp nose she had once been a beautiful woman with a bright smile. Now fat had ruined her and ruined her marriage as well, for Tim Aina had finally become bored of those pouches of fat. The sight of all these young girls with slim or plump bodies had finally lured him into cheating. Her hands were thick, legs as fat as timber and middle with enough fat to drown a whale. When she moved, she dragged herself like a trailer sweeping all before her.

She swept over to the telephone, scooped it up in her chubby hands and dialled Tim's office number. She waited for some time and dialled again, the ringing down the line and the ominous silence making her heart beat accelerate rapidly. Satisfied that no answer was forthcoming she dialled Police Headquarters. Maybe the chief of police would do something. He was Tim's friend.

A deep voice came over the line. "Hello. Police Corporal, Jim Okuns."

"Hello! Dupe Aina. Can you put me through to the Chief of Police?"

"Sorry miss. I. . . . ."

"Madam."

"Sorry Madam. Forgive the mistake. I tend to make wrong assumptions sometimes."

"Okay, okay." She said impatiently. "What about the chief of Police?"

"Left for home half an hour ago."

There was a moment's silence down the line as she considered her next line of action.

"You still there, Madam?"

"Yes. Can you put me through to his residence? I'd want a few words with him.''

At the end of the line Corporal Jim Okuns cleared his throat nervously, searching for the right words for this occasion. He knew that this woman had to be handled with kids' gloves. She just could be a friend of his boss and she could put in a bad word for him.

"Well. . .er. . . Madam, the boss said not to disturb him. Said I should handle all calls for him except if there's a murder case. He's been working like a mule for the past seventeen hours without a wink of sleep and sure needs the rest. Besides, my arse would be in a frying pan if I disobeyed orders.''

"I understand your position Corporal, but you don't worry about this. This Chief's a personal friend of mine. He would be so happy to hear from me he wouldn't remember you existed.''

"But madam if you want a private chat with him you could use his home number. That would save a lot of trouble.''

"This isn't what you would exactly call a private chat.'' Dupe said in a condescending tone. "My husband has not returned from work since morning. This is unusual of him. I have phoned his office two times without any reply. Could be he's missing.''

Jim Okuns laughed politely into the telephone. "It's still too early to declare him missing. He's probably on his way home now. This isn't surprising. Unusual things happen once in a while. If he isn't back by ten, then call me back. We may have something for you then.''

Dupe stiffened. "What do you mean by 'we may have something for you then?' ''

"Aw. . . . . well some big trouble somewhere this evening. Some of our men have gone out to investigate. If your husband isn't back, then there is just a slight chance he might be involved in the trouble.''

Dupe flinched, cold sweat beginning to run down her fat face. Her palms were moist and shaking so that she had difficulty in holding the phone. The thought that her husband had gotten into some big trouble turned her sick with fear. She had to get to the Police Chief quick. The remembrance that there could be help in this direction tightened her guts.

"I must speak to your boss.'' She said with new resolve. "This is important."

Jim Okuns was getting impatient at her obstinacy and he made no effort to hide it. "Well, madam I wouldn't advise this. When the Chief went home this evening, his eyes were red and swollen from lack of sleep. I'm sure he wouldn't want even his mother to disturb him now."

"Look corporal!" Her voice suddenly hardened. "When I say I want the Chief then I want the Chief. Understand? Okay I want the Chief! Raise him from the dead if you have to! And heaven help you if I have to raise him myself." She paused to take in a deep breath. "I'll have your rotten arse in that frying pan you dread so much."

"Enough madam. I obey orders to the letter. I have my job to think of."

"Sod you and your stinking job! Get him!" She couldn't imagine what made this self-conceited corporal think his job was more important than her husband.

"Okay woman, you asked for it. Know what I think? You've fallen from grace. When a man starts coming home late from work he's got a better frill to take care of him. Your husband is possibly in some woman's arms now, probably a whore. Imagine competing with a whore!" He laughed in a harsh, sarcastic way. "Well, cheer up." And he banged the phone down.

C

There were four of them in the room; four hard-core criminals who shared a common purpose. They had all gathered for an important occasion, so the bottle of whisky on the table was to prepare themselves for it.

Ify Madu was the only female in the room and she lay on a small hard bed, flipping aimlessly through a magazine. She was bored with the waiting and impatient to lay hands on her cut of the take. The grisly end of Tim Aina had only Shocked her that moment, but four hours had elapsed since the killing and it was ample time for her to forget him and concentrate on her share of the take.

She needed money badly. Her shoes were old and worn out, well past the salvage value. Even most of her clothes were out of fashion — Joe hadn't bought any for her recently. In fact he too was running out of cash.

Then the door creaked opened and the deadliest of them came in. He was two inches past the six feet rod and wearing a false smile as he lumbered in. This was the one called Gilt Jimoh.

Gilt Jimoh! Aeunuch! The man who was incapable of being sexually aroused. A man? Well you couldn't possibly call this lump of sexually lifeless flesh a man. You couldn't call him a man when women had no use for him. He was just an impotent lump of flesh.

His head was big and oval in shape, sharp eyes as large as saucers. The nose stood broadly at the centre of a face that had knife scars — scars he had accumulated from knife brawls over the years. When he spoke his jaws moved slowly so that the large mouth barely opened. His voice wasn't deep but it had a musical lilt to it which had once landed him in a recording studio.

Jimoh paused beside the table where the three other men were playing cards.

At the head of the table was Joe Puna, an ex-soldier who had been driven from the military for swindling. He loved violence especially when it meant brutalizing his juniors and was endeared to fast living, women and booze. In his late thirties, he was slim with closely cropped hair and mean, hard eyes. When you looked at his washed-out eyes you categorised him as one of the men who had killed many times before and needed little pressure to kill again.

Furo Kpondo on Joe's right was a weather-beaten character. Small and ageing he had served a ten year stretch for manslaughter after which he took a two year rap for forgery. He had a big beaky nose with a sharp mind for facts. The grey on his temples said he had seen fifty already.

Lastly, on Joe's left was the flashy guy who called himself Bill Young. He loved fancy clothes and well-cut shoes with a huge inherited appetite for sex. He had raped his sister at the age of sixteen, dropped out of school and started roaming about, picking pockets and finally burgling houses. He had served a year in jail where he learnt how to live flashily and talk big. On coming out, he had raped and murdered a teenage girl who hawked oranges, and running from the police he had met Jimoh, who hid him until the heat died down and during that time taught the youngster how to use guns. Bill had a knack for guns and he was now one of the most feared shots in the Benin underworld. Tall, slim and lively he was the most handsome of the lot. His head was finely shaped, eyes a dreamy grey and the well-cut defiant nose made him more captivating to girls. With his lovely chin, dark sideboards and flashy ways you wouldn't know this young man was a crook. He had just struck twenty-two.

Gilt Jimoh gave them one of his false smiles. "I apologise for keeping you guys waiting. Couldn't help seeing to something urgent. We're going to proceed with haste." He paused to glance at the briefcase lying on the table. "That the money?"

Joe nodded, then grinned. "Everything went as planned. We've counted the money. Four thousand bread. Just as you said."

Joe and Bill had carried out the remaining operation from where Ify stopped. After killing Aina they had left him there in the bush and driven to this place in the Rover as quickly as possible. This was Furo Kpondo's joint where they usually met after jobs.

Jimoh drew the briefcase towards him. He glanced at the pile of money inside, nodded and slid the lid shut. Then he drew out a chair and sat down.

"Aren't you counting the money?" Ify asked as she sidled over to sit on the edge of the table. She was surprised because Jimoh never sat down without counting any take.

"Not necessary." He said. "I wouldn't send you guys on such an operation if I didn't trust you. Moreover I think we can put our time to better use." Jimoh stopped, the false smile playing around the corners of his mouth as he glanced around at his audience. He liked the lights of expectation in their eyes. It meant they felt that something big was brewing. He continued: "You guys must have guessed that something big was smouldering, though I have only hinted about it to Joe. I have reserved the bombshell for an occasion like this, when everyone would be present."

"Okay then," Ify said, "before the drama starts, let's split this bread here. My shoes are getting old. I want to buy new ones."

"There isn't going to be any split." Jimoh announced with finality.

"What do you mean by 'there isn't going to be any split?' " Furo Kpondo chipped in, his eyes hardening. "Don't start getting ideas about making off with all the bread. We've all worked for it so I guess each of us is entitled to his cut. No one is leaving here alive with my cut." For emphasis he placed a .38 Police Special on the table, his finger closed over the trigger.

Jimoh laughed. "Put away that gun. I don't like guns when I'm speaking. They make me nervous."

"My bread is more important to me. If not for my experience you might have succeeded in conning me. All along I've been alert. I knew that one day a smart guy in this gang would dream about making away with the result of our sweat."

"Come on, be sensible Furo!" Jimoh's false smile was slipping off, being replaced by an impatient line on his mouth. "When I say no split I mean no split. We're going to need this bread for the last stroke."

The others in the room rubbed their palms nervously, eyeing each other uneasily. It was Young who found his voice first.

"You planning a coup or something?"

"Something like that." The false smile was back by now. "This is going to be the coup of the century."

"For God's sake!" Joe exclaimed. "You can't be torturing us like this Gilt. Give us what's on your mind. If there's going to be a coup then let us in on the beans before we die from high blood pressure."

Jimoh mopped his brow with a grubby handkerchief, adjusted the collar of his shirt and looked around, a strange light in his eyes. "We've been fools all along, " he began, "going after chicken-feed when there were rams to be had. A hundred bread is nothing but we've gone after it several times. Smart Joe has killed two men before for a couple of hundred naira. Have you ever asked yourself what you are going to do when you grow old? Have you ever paused to ask why you've been risking your neck for a couple of hundred naira when there are millions to be had?" He paused to moisten his lips. "Okay, so we've been fools all along; our luck wouldn't hold out forever. So why don't we carry out the last steal, call it quits and get out of this sodden business?"

"A good idea." Kpondo said. "I'm tired of being on the wanted list of many cops throughout the country. So what's your last steal Gilt? We going to rob a gold mine?"

"Something like that. I have had this idea for sometime but only gave it a serious thought recently. With one and a half million naira shared we could afford to call it quits."

"Phew!" Young whistled. "With that kind of bread I can go have myself a ball on the moon till the rest of my days. But surely, one and a half million isn't what we can pick from the gutter."

"There's money in Nigeria. Lots of it. Oil money, and we own the oil. Crisp naira bills, being allowed to waste in banks. There's the Bendel State Bank — one of the richest banks in this country. What stops us stealing a million and half and splitting the take? There's more than enough there so they won't miss the bread." Kpondo relaxed visibly and even managed to laugh. "What's this? If it isn't a pipe dream then you surely have been soaking booze."

"There's nothing so crazy in robbing a bank, is there? Lots of guys have robbed banks before and some have gotten away with it."

"Yeah. Lucky chaps they were, to rob banks and get away with it. Why didn't they try the Bendel State Bank? A couple of banks around here don't keep much bread in their vaults at night so their security is lax. Guys rob these banks and boast. This Bendel State Bank is sheer class. Lots of bread in that vault so the security there is complex and water-tight. Look, I've dreamed before of robbing this bank. I nursed this dream until Big Ben and his mob raided the bank one dark night. He was slain with eight members of his gang. If you imagine we can rob this bank you have another thinking coming."

"We're going to rob this bank if it's the last thing we do." Jimoh said calmly. He had anticipated that there would be serious opposition to this scheme so he'd come prepared. "As I said before this is going to be the last stroke. We can't continue stealing forever. After this I am calling it quits. Now let me . . . ."

He was cut off by Puna's interruption. "Gilt, I think Furo is right. What you are saying is probably a pipe dream. Robbing big banks isn't like taking money from lazy old men."

"You're smart, Joe, aren't you? For one long year we've been pulling off jobs together. All this time have you ever heard me putting forward a job we couldn't swing?"

"No Gilt, but robbing this bank is something different. A witch couldn't rob this bank. Robbing old men is like taking sweets from children. But in this we are up against professionals and a complex security system. Could be you are slipping up for once."

"Let's hear what Gilt has got to say. We can't condemn a plan without hearing the outline." Ify got off the edge of the table, swinging her cheap handbag. She was eager for Jimoh to explain his strategy for robbing that bank. Could be the slick eunuch had come up with some clever plan to outwit the brains behind the security system of that bank. Sure, she could do with that bread. A million and a half split in five would land her three hundred thousand.

Three hundred thousand! The thought of all this money made her heart lurch.

Jimoh looked at her and managed a genuine smile. "Thanks. As I said before I wouldn't bring forward a job I knew couldn't come off. I don't gamble. Have implicit faith in me and . . . ."

"Look bud, Big Ben failed." Furo piped in stubbornly. "And where Big Ben failed no one . . . ."

"Stop all this shit about Big Ben!" Ify hissed, glaring at him furiously. "What about it if Big Ben failed? If any man is going to rob that bank then Gilt is that man."

"Yeah, I'm that man." Gilt added as if there had been no interruption. "For sometime I have watched that bank – all the goings in and out. All we have to do is rob that bank while the guards are sleeping and make a quick get-away. Plus some false trails for the cops."

"But you're just telling us the result of the operation, not the outline of the plans." Furo persisted.

"I know. Before I explain the details of the plan I have got to know who is with me. Can't risk anyone backing out later. If anyone wants to back out, let him do so now."

No one made any move. If the scheme was going to come off, everyone wanted to be in favour then. Looking at them Jimoh suddenly grinned.

"I take it some of you are skeptical but don't want to be on the losing side in the event there is success. I'm assuring you all that this plan is fool proof so I don't want anyone becoming chicken-hearted at the last minute. If this plan's going to succeed everyone has got to be in or out from the beginning." He paused to wipe the drool that was appearing at the right corner of his mouth and directed his gaze on Furo, his eyes glittering. "I am particularly worried about you Furo. You in with me or out?"

Furo grimaced, then grinned. "Count me in. I guess if that bank's got to be robbed you'll be the person to do it. An old man like me has got nothing to lose. No one will miss me."

"Good. Bill?"

Bill raised his thumb. "In."

Jimoh began to grin. The only guy remaining who could refuse was Joe Puna. He knew that any day Ify would jump up at such an idea so he could safely assume her response as positive.

"What about you, Smarty?" He asked, using Joe's favourite sobriquet.

"I don't know. How about Ify?"

"Me? I'm in." She uttered with incredulity.

Joe shrugged. "Well if she's in, then count me in. I have nothing to lose either."

Jimoh's smile widened. "Beautiful." He said. "I knew I could rely on you guys anyday. When the money is split, each of us will get two hundred and fifty thousand naira. A lot of bread. Can serve anyong for the rest of his . . . ."

"Two hundred and fifty thousand?" Ify's sharp voice was accusing. "A million and half split in five gives three hundred thousand."

Jimoh frowned. "Yeah. I forgot to tell you. There's a sixth person involved in this business."

He rapped on the table three times. The door opened and the man swaggered into the room.

II

A

Corporal Jim Okuns rubbed his eyes and yawned widely.

"You trying to swallow me or something?" Detective Omo Baba asked, shrinking away from him in mock fright.

"Could be. I sure could do with your fat nose for a start."

Corporal Jim Okuns was short and thick set. His large dome of a head was set squarely on the thick neck. He had the hard no-nonsense face of a cop who had to start from scratch and an aggresive jaw and he walked with the springy steps of a panther. He was as hairy as an ape.

On the table were two telephones — one for internal communication and the other was connected to external lines. Then an elaborate two-way radio control set was directly in front of him from where he could communicate with the squad cars patrolling the city. This radio network was a new gimmick at police headquarters. The Police Commissioner had been forced to order for it when the citizens of the City started yelling about the alarming rate of crime upswing. The Force was being handicapped by inadequate staff coupled with the inefficiency of communication networks (most public telephones in the City were either out of working order or the lines busy). Cops on the beat couldn't report any emergency quickly so that necessary action could be taken and criminals were cashing in on this. But with this radio around, criminals weren't having it easy.

Detective Oma Baba, who had come into the room to share

some cigarettes with Okuns was a slender cop in his early thirties, six feet tall and he had a narrow face with thin lips. When he let his gaze fall on someone it was in a disconcerting way that made the fellow shift his eyes. He was a cop of immense pride and confidence, hence his walk was a disdainful swagger. He never hurried except in an emergency. Being the best shot at police headquarters, his confidence was justified.

Omo Baba liked living well more than anything. A greedy, dishonest cop, he used his badge to enrich himself. He usually blackmailed pimps and prostitutes into paying 'shut up' money to him. He took bribes, coerced criminals for bread and knew most hot spots in town where he could make a couple of naira every night. But he was a very efficient cop.

"Anything in the wind?" He asked Okuns, drawing out a chair as he spoke. News interested him. He picked out most things in the wind and used them to his advantage.

Okuns shrugged. "Little, but it could blow into a scandal. A woman said her name was Dupe Aina, phoned to report that her husband was missing. Wanted me to ring the boss and get him out of sleep. Said she's a friend to the boss. I explained to her that the boss handn't seen a wink of sleep for sometime, that he would demand my arse raw if I disturbed his sleep. Then she got nasty and threatened me. Said if I didn't give in to her demand she would see to it personally that my arse never escaped the frying pan." He paused, squinted at Baba to see whether he was still listening, then laughed loud. "Know what I think? Her husband is somewhere screwing a cheap whore. And I told her so, then banged down the phone."

He looked at Baba, his eyes shinning with glee that he had flung one of the rich into the dust. Baba shook out a cigarette, lit it and offered him the pack. He blew smoke rings at the ceiling for sometime, then stared at Okuns.

"I wouldn't advise you to cross any of the boss's friend. If that woman's her friend as she claimed to be, your arse is in one hell of a frying pan."

"The boss can't do me nothing. I was merely obeying orders. As for the 'slip' about her husband and a whore, I don't think she would mention it to the boss. If she does, it's her word against mine."

"Your funeral, not mine." He paused to inhale another gale of smoke. "Know what I think? This city's going to explode any minute."

"What makes you think so?"

"A dream. I've never dreamt in the afternoon before. But this afternoon, while I was dozing in a chair I dreamt that the city was going to explode soon. And mark my words Jim, it's going to explode any minute. My dreams are sort of visions."

"You coming with your wild crazy dreams again? Don't let the chief hear your opinion of them or you'll be kicked out of the Force."

Grinning broadly, Baba shrugged and got out of the chair. "Call them wild and crazy if you like, but mark them. Could be one day I'll dream about becoming the chief of police and WHAM, before you know it, I am occupying Ogunbor's seat. I'll see a fortune teller tomorrow. He might have something for.........."

Just then the radio crackled into life.

"Squad five calling. Squad five calling. Hello. Hello..........."

Okuns turned up the volume, pressed down a green switch and took up the mike.

"Yeah? Yeah? Headquarters here. Headquarters here. Eagle skin ready to receive."

"This is Sergeant Phil Jumbo reporting. I repeat. Sergeant Phil Jumbo reporting. We've found a body in the bush. A man. Probably dead. Half his brains sticking out of his skull. Send the doctor and ambulance along. We'll stand by."

Okuns cursed inside his throat. Sod the sergeant to try teaching him his job. Or did being a Sergeant make one arrogant when he was talking to a junior officer? Nevertheless he asked, "Location?"

"Junction 15. Near the highway to Lagos. Our blue light will be on. Okay?"

"Yeah. Thanks. Over."

Okuns clamped back the mike, pressed the green switch further so that it came all the way up. He swivelled to grin at Baba who was still rooted to the spot where he'd been standing before the message came in. "Could be you are right about this city exploding. The boss will go crazy if this dead man is who I think he is."

He picked up the phone that was marked internal, rang the Police doctor and ambulance attendants up and informed them of what was in the wind. As he clamped down the receiver and made for the other phone, Baba grinned.

"Going to raise the boss?"

"Yeah. Said I should do so only in the event of murder. From what that Serge said, this has got to be nothing but murder. A man can't dream of becoming Chief of Police with half his brains sticking out of his head."

Baba lost his grin. "Watch your mouth mister!" he warned, a cold threatening look on his face. "If this gets to the Chief I'll raise hell for you that being kicked out from the force will be a welcome break."

With this he shuffled out of the room, banged the door with disdain and went plodding down the stairs to his squad car.

B

He was a neatly dressed man of average height in his middle thirties, sporting a goatee. Lean and with eyes a baby grey, you could easily mistake him for an innocent monk on the road. But this man was very deadly. Brian Obi was formerly manager of the Bendel State Bank — he had been retired during the mass purge by the Federal Military Government for 'unaccountability of public funds.' He had escaped going to jail by a hair's breadth. Since then Obi had set out carefully to rob this bank, making a cautious but exhaustive inquiry about the mobs operating in town. On hearing about Jimoh's gang he had quickly concluded that here was his gang. No other gang was best suited for this job. So he had set about tracing Jimoh and putting forward his plans to him. Jimoh had been enthusiastic about it. All that remained then was to convince his gang.

As he strode into the room. Jimoh glanced around, beaming with an air of importance. He made an introductory gesture with his hands. "The former Manager of Bendel State Bank, Mr. Brian Obi. The sixth and most important member in this last stroke. A very agreeable man as you'll see." He paused to pull out a worn-out chair for the former Bank Manager. "And Mr. Obi, I am glad to introduce to you the deadliest criminals one can find in this evil city." Using his forefinger to indicate who he meant, "Joe Puna, Furo Kpondo, Ify Madu, Bill Young."

Obi shook hands with everyone and, still smiling, sat down on the chair.

"I'm going to continue from where I stopped before." Jimoh began smoothly again. "But I'll hasten to add that most of the information at my disposal is due to the courtesy of our friend Obi. If there is anything any of you don't understand, don't hesitate to ask questions." He paused, glanced at the expectant faces gathered round the table as if trying to draw inspiration from them, then rattled on more smoothly. "During the day, this bank is guarded by four seasoned policemen. We could knock off these guards and carry out a hold-up but many guys are always around the bank at this time that one could possibly slip away and alert the police. Moreover I don't fancy daylight robberies. People can always identify you even if you are masked. But the most important point against it is that Police Headquarters is just two stone throws from the bank. In broad daylight our car can easily be identified and trailed so the chance of getting away with people staring at us is mininal. I'm merely trying to rule out any possibility of the operation being carried out in broad daylight so that the issue will not become a bone of contention and much rangling.

This means that the operation can only be carried out at night. But then more formidable security measures are arraigned against us. At 5 pm. the bank closes down. Just before the Manager leaves, two squads, one of twelve police men and the other of twelve soldiers arrive to take over the human aspect of the security at the bank. The Bank Manager is escorted by the other four cops to Police Headquarters where he dumps the bank keys with the

Chief of Police. Meanwhile those twenty-four guards keep watch over the Bank until eight o'clock. At eight p.m. the soldiers go over to the little canteen beside the bank where they have their supper. After them, then it's the turn of the Policemen to eat their's while the soldiers resume watch. Make no mistake about this, these guards are probably the most trained and best equipped of all the lousy guards in this state. From five p.m. till eight a.m. the following morning, they keep a very alert, steady watch on the bank with a little interruption coming at supper time. Even then, with their strength halved, they are still unbeatable." He stopped and leered at his enthralled audience. "Any questions so far?"

Furo nodded. "I don't suppose you are planning that we take on these twenty-four tough nuts?"

"We've not yet come to that." Jimoh replied curtly, then rambled on. "Lastly, the supper that is served to those guards is prepared by a policewoman. This is done at her quarters. She is trusted by both the police and the bank. Her loyalty is unswerving, otherwise they wouldn't have given her the job. But there is a flaw here which we can use to our advantage. She's ugly and lonely.

Now we move over to the electronics aspect of the security network. To enter the bank one has to pass through two doors — an outer and inner door. Both are double swing doors. The former is of solid oak, not likely to yield to any battering unless you blow it open and that will be heard from Police Headquarters. If you try to pick the lock, an alarm will go off and can alert those creeps at Police Headquarters. The latter door is of glass and similar to the first one — any gimmick and the alarm will go off except when you use the key. If you break the glass this will trigger off an explosion that is injurious and even if you escape injury the cops from headquarters will be around in a minute." He paused to wipe sweat that was streaming down his broad face.

"Then we come to the last obstacle assuming one has crossed the other obstacles. The vault is underground, with a flight of stairs leading to it. At the bottom of the stairs is the vault door made of the strongest metals that existed. It's not for me to dabble into the chemistry of the door. A minor explosive can't blow open that vault door. You have to use armour piercing shells like that from Bazooka

Shells. Even then this will not only set an alarm off, the blast in itself would alert the cops. This then leaves no alternative except the vault key. Any gimmicks . . . . the alarm. If you are able to enter the vault you can help yourself to the finest haul of cash you'll ever hope to see."

Joe stared at him, trying to control the outburst that was welling up in him. At last. "So you know all the aspects of this security complex and still imagine you can swing it? You going demented or something?"

"Don't rush things!" Furo hastened to snap at him. "He has just finished presenting the obstacles in our path. Give him a chance to put forward his plan." He paused to see how Jimoh was responding, nodded to acknowledge his thanks then continued. "But I have a point that needs explained to me." He looked at Jimoh with wise eyes. "How is it that we are going to get only one and a half million Naira from that bank? It is supposed to be one of the richest banks in the country."

Jimoh shrugged. "It could be more or less. The bank keeps its reserves with the branch of the Central Bank here. It is not for me to decide the bleeding sum they should have at their bank." He was avoiding Furo's eyes as he spoke. The guy's wise eyes disconcerted him. It could well be that the most experienced criminal working with him was beginning to suspect what he and Obi had agreed on.

"It's not like you, Gilt, to suggest getting the same share as us. How come you decide that each person would get two hundred and fifty thousand when you've actually been doing some groundwork? You planning to add more salt in your stew or something?"

There was a wave of laughter round the table and when Jimoh finally forced himself to meet Furo's eyes, dangerous lights were smouldering in his eyes.

"You mind your business and I'll mind mine. What of it if I decide to put more salt in my stew? You've never seen ten thousand all your blooming life, so why bother a man who is throwing two-hundred and fifty thousand into your laps?"

"Okay, forget it. But you shouldn't have pretended to be so innocent."

Jimoh glared at him then resumed the planning. "Getting back to the subject of discussion, I am entitled to believe that everyone is now acquinted with the obstacles in our path so we now move on to the robbery itself. As some of you might have guessed, the operation has got to be carried out not only with minimum noise if we've got to avoid the cops but with maximum caution. Any irresponsible act can trigger off alarms which means the whole operation is bungled. Therefore for simplicity I'm going to split the whole operation into four parts so that each part can be accomplished differently."

"The first part is how to dispose of the guards. You can't dislodge those guards easily even if you came at them with a tank so we have to look for a simple way of incapacitating them. This is where Bill starts earning his share of the steal." He grinned broadly at the expectant faces gathered round the table and plunged on again. "You have a situation you think is almost impossible to overcome, look for the simple solutions and WHAM the problem seems then like taking sweets from a kid. The policewoman who prepares supper for the guards is ugly and lonely. Men ignore her as if she didn't exist and someone has called her repulsive before. Bill will play up to her; make her believe you dig her. It's up to you, the method you use in convincing her but she should have no cause to suspect your motive. You're young and handsome and she's ugly and unwanted so she'll surely fall for you. You should be around when she's preparing the supper. When she's ready give her something that will make her forget the supper. You'll probably have to screw her. While you are doing it. Ify will pass through another door which you must have left open before. The food should be in the kitchen and she would dope it with whatever I give her. There must be no trace of the drugs on the food else those guards wouldn't touch it." He halted to regard his audience with his false smile. "Following me so far?"

Bill grinned at him. "You sure are a great criminal genius. Wouldn't cost me a dime to screw that broad. If past experience's anything to go by then she'll be difficult to satisfy."

Jimoh winked at him, then continued. "When she takes the food to the guards you stay in her house and think up an easy way of killing her without alerting the neighbourhood. Use a silent weapon.

There's to be no fingerprints left behind. I don't have to tell you that knocking her off is vitally important. She's a well trained cop so bungle it and any day she can point the finger at you."

Bill's jaw went slack. "Kill her?" He querried softly as if he hadn't heard right. "Look, it's easy to kill someone you don't know or who means nothing to you. But to knock off a dame you've just laid is no longer my cup of tea."

Jimoh waved his hand impatiently. "Please yourself. You are earning two-hundred and fifty thousand, not a couple of Naira. You've got to work for it. A man can't climb a mountain without sweating."

"If the woman is so love-hungry as you say, why bother to knock her off when I can make her to work for us. Give her a chance to live and you'll see how I'll handle her."

"I don't like loose ends. That end has got to be wrapped up completely." Suddenly his eyes turned to chips of ice as he stared at Bill, making the youngster's arrogant confidence slip away. "If that woman sees a wink of daylight after that robbery, then you become a dangerous liability and expendable. You and your lover will perish in a fire accident."

"Easy, Gilt." Joe's breath came out in a controlled gasp. "Go easy with the lad. He will knock her off for sure. He couldn't possibly hope to lay his hands on such a pile anywhere if this chance slips through his fingers. Go ahead with the plans. We're still listening."

"Okay. I'm sorry for going hard on him. So the guards are doped. The drugs take effect after two hours and they fall asleep. Meanwhile Bill has knocked off the cop woman. Then the second part of the operation comes into play — entering the vault. Mr. Obi has got the keys to the oak door, to the glass door and finally the vault. He had the keys cast from the originals while he was still the Bank's Manager. He will direct this stage of the operation and each person has got to conduct himself well. A mistake and the cops will be swarming the bank before we know it. Once inside we help ourselves to the crates of bread there. After this comes the third part of our operation — the get-away. I don't envisage any trouble but we've got to be prepared for it so that in the event it occurs,

we are not found wanting. There just could be a little bungling
and the cops are alerted before our get-away. They would be looking
for a robber's vehicle but not an ambulance definitely. So, just
before we raid the bank, Furo goes over to the hospital to bring the
ambulance. This we will use for our get-away. Still following me?"

"Don't you think the plan is becoming too complicated?" Ify
asked. "You seem to be worrying too much about small items."

"Yeah? It's the small items that count. Great criminals fail
because when they have everything working for them, they tend to
neglect the small items. When something as big as a million Naira
is at stake you've got to plan for every emergency. If in the unlikely
event that something happens, you've got to be prepared for it.
When we get away, there would be no need coming back here so
we proceed to the new apartment, the one I showed you guys
yesterday."

"Phew!" Furo whistled, then grinned. "You're the greatest criminal that ever trod Nigerian soil. Given a thousand years I couldn't
have dreamt up such a plan."

Jimoh's heart swelled at the compliment. He liked being praised,
especially when he had just come up with a master-plan. He smiled
a genuine smile.

"I haven't finished yet." He said."As I told you guys before I
don't leave loose ends. Everything has got to be wrapped and tied
like a package. The cops in this city are no mugs like some of us say
offhandedly sometimes. Once an investigation starts, they will
know it's an internal job. Nobody robs that bank without detailed
first-hand information. Mr. Obi could be in trouble once the investigation starts. Someone just might mention the 'former Bank
Manager' and the cops would latch unto him like a leech. So we've
got to give them a false lead. One of the men who work at the bank
is going to disappear. His girl friend lives with him so we have no
choice — the two should go together. Joe this is your job. You
and Ify will knock those two guys off on the night of the robbery —
better before the robbery because after that, things could become
very hot. As I have emphasized before, little noise, so no guns. We
don't want the cops to be alerted. I'll see two of you later so that
we can work out the detailed plans. Any questions before we call

it a night?"

Ify cleared her throat nervously. "Look Gilt, the killings are too much. Three bodies in one night! I don't want to be present at two more killings. They make me sick." Though she didn't say it, she was secretly worried at the prospect of having to participate in the killings herself.

Jimoh stared at her uncompromisingly. "You don't lay hands on two-hundred and fifty thousand by sitting on the fence and watching others earn it. You've got to participate. You're going to be involved in this like the rest of us. Under Joe's supervision, you're going to kill that man's girl friend. Understand?"

"Sod it..!" Joe shouted. "Seems you're going nutty, Gilt. Don't you realize that we're merely complicating issues for ourselves by knocking off that pair! The Police can suspect Brian if they like. Suspicion isn't proof. They've got to have enough before they can lay hands on him. Besides he may not participate in the actual robbery. He can stay at home or with friends . . . . have an alibi."

Obi gave him a bland look. "Friend, I've got the keys to that bank. No one knows where those keys are. My position is dicey. Before I bring out these keys, I have got to be sure those two guys are dead and missing. And when I say dead and missing, I mean dead and buried. If this condition is not met, then no robbery."

Jimoh grinned. "Well, you've heard it from the horse's mouth. Either we play with him or no robbery." He paused, then resumed. "I forgot to remind you guys of something. You wanted to know what the four thousand you grabbed today will be used for. As I mentioned before, I have hired a new apartment. The Land-lady has demanded two thousand as a year's rent in advance. We need that apartment. It's out of town, quiet and houses no other oc-cupants. We're going to buy provisions, drinks for celebration and some household furniture. The place has got to look like an ideal home in case a smart cop stumbles into the apartment any day. We are going to live like comrades so Furo wouldn't be using this hole for some time. As I told you before I'm not leaving anything to chance. I'm prepared for almost all emergencies. Just do what I tell you, everything will be all right." He yawned. "It has been a night. I am tired. Let's go sleep?"

"Wait a minute!" Joe said sharply. "You've been rambling on for hours. This plan is slip-shod and hurried. We don't even know when the robbery is taking place. Why not go over the whole operation again?"

Jimoh pushed back his chair and stood up. "I've deliberetely left out when the robbery is taking place. We'll meet again tomorrow at dawn. Then we can finalise plans, polish up the slippery parts and set the plans in motion."

III

A

Mike Buko leaned on the balcony rail, his body bared to the cool night breeze. He watched the traffic on the road absentmindedly, wondering about how life would be without cars, lights, clothes . . . . while the breeze whispered in his ear. There would be no glamour in life, he mused to himself. Glamour? Did the stone age people experience any thrill in life . . . .?

He was in his mid-twenties, a university graduate in Business Management. Lean, with a long narrow face and bushy hair he was nearly five-eleven. This young man was one of the new graduates of business with high ambitions and high hopes of hitting the limelight very soon. He had only been with the Bendel State Bank for a year as the Assistant Financial Manager of the bank.

Buko was engaged to a dark beauty called Pat Ola. They were due to marry in a month's time. He was a man of high tastes who liked people to be impressed by his way with things, which was only a way of hitting the limelight. To enhance this image, he was preparing a lavish marriage ceremony which would be talked about for a long time. Despite his outward showmanship, he was inwardly a realist. He knew he was heading for a financial debacle but his pride and the image he was creating wouldn't allow him reduce the budget for the ceremony.

As he leaned on the balcony rail, turning the ceremony in his mind, he became aware of a shadow falling beside him. Startled, he whipped around only to find it was his financee

"Ah, it's you." He said, relaxing. "You frightened me, love. I was almost startled."

Pat came into his arms. She was small, with a toothy smile and almond-shaped hypnotic eyes. She had a small firm behind, slim legs and well manicured nails. When you look at the upward thrust of her breasts, the tantalising heaving against the fabric she was wearing, you would feel breathless and sigh like someone under a hypnotic spell. And hypnotised Buko was. From the moment he met her he was hooked.

This night she was wearing only a flowing negligee that clung perfectly to her curves, making Buko's mouth water. "Let's go inside, Mike." She said, nuzzling his lips. "You've been outside for sometime now. I want you to come and dance with me."

He followed her into the sitting-room where light rock music was playing. He hated dancing at night but didn't tell her so. Instead, he said. "Let's do something better than dancing."

"And what will that be?" For an answer he grabbed her, covering her with flaming kisses and making her moan with pleasure. He lifted her off her feet, carried her over to the sofa and laid her down gently as if afraid of hurting her. Their tongues met again, moist and hot at the area of contact. He could feel her tongue inside him — quick, darting messages of her desire and passion. Seeking, probing and finding. He could also feel the heat inside her being unbottled. He wasn't sure of what his fingers were doing — feeling, snaking and bringing those expectant moans from her. Then they were tugging at the negligee, trying to flip it over her head.

"No, Mike, no." She said softly in a weakened voice. Her eyes said Yes. Her body and soul said yes but her mouth was offering weak nos.

He smiled down warmly at her, his eyes telling her that he knew she wanted it badly — that the meek resistance was to be expected. His eyes told her more — that he was going to give it to her now, that he too wanted it badly. As he began to undress her, there was loud persistent knocking on the door.

Mike swore softly under his breath and made to release her.

"Don't answer the door." She pleaded. "Please."

He grinned, blew her a quick kiss and got up from the sofa. "Let's see the person first. When the guy goes we can continue from where we stopped."

Walking to the door, he slid back the bolt and opened it. And there was the towering eunuch before him.

"Good evening." Jimoh greeted, smothering him with his eyes. "How do you do?"

Buko was slightly puzzled. He had never seen this man before, yet the guy was behaving like someone who knew him. "Come in. Come in." He said, standing aside to allow Jimoh pass. "I don't seem to have had the pleasure of your acquaintance before?"

Jimoh allowed his false smile to come into play. "Could be we've met. Could be we've not. But in my world of business, physical meeting is only a round-off of the various metaphysical meetings that have been taking place." He selected the most comfortable lounging chair in the room and sat down with much fuss. "I'm Charles Okala. Boss of Okala Transport Limited. I suppose you're Mike Buko?"

Buko nodded. He was beginning to feel a little inferior. This Okala with his rich superior manners slightly overwhelmed him. He didn't want to switch on the usual rich impression of himself on this occasion. He had the sickening feeling it was going to bounce off this man like a golf ball. However he tried to establish his presence.

"Said you're Mr. Okala, boss of Okala Transport Limited? Don't seem to have heard of that Company before."

Jimoh, wearing a well-cut business suit smiled at him contemptuously. He fished out a pack of rich cigars, shook out one and lit it. "Permit me." He said, allowing his gaze to wander around the room and settle finally on Pat. "A chronic habit of mine. Can't discuss business without a smoke." He blew smoke towards Pat. "A fine lady you've got there."

Buko's narrow face broke into a grin. Flattery was to him what meat is to a lion. Flatter him a little and you have him hooked.

"I know." He said, beginning to shed his inferiority complex. "She's sheer class. When I go for anything it's for class." He paused. "But this business you're talking about . . . . go on."

Jimoh dragged on the cigar, inhaled deeply and let out a stream of smoke through his nose. He nodded at Pat. "Tell your woman to leave us for some minutes. When I talk business, I don't like my eyes to be wandering."

Pat glanced at Mike and seeing him nod, got up reluctantly and walked away with her firm behind shaking a little provocatively. At the door to her bedroom, she stopped to lean on the frame. Turning her head she looked at Jimoh with an obstinate frown. She flinched at the cold, murderous look in Jimoh's eyes and quickly bolted into the bedroom.

Jimoh, pleased at having scared her, turned his attention to Buko again. "You're Mike Buko. Assistant Financial Manager of the Bendel State Bank. A chum recommended you. Said you're one of the best brains in Financial Business — that for this venture of mine I wouldn't find a better guy." He threw down another gale of smoke, staring at his bait. The broad smile on Mike's face pleased him. A little flattery before he dangled the bait. Okay here goes: "As for my business, I own Okala Transport Limited. Consists of a fleet of buses. We're not old in the Transport business; could be the reason why you've not heard of us. But we're expanding fast . . . . ."

Buko interrupted him. "This chum of yours, who made the recommendation . . . . who's he? What's his name?"

Jimoh made an impatient gesture with his hand. "Someone you know. I prefer to refer to him as a chum. When I discuss business I keep out as many names as possible."

Buko stared at him for a long suspicious moment, then shrugged. "Okay, call him chum or anything you like. Guess it's no skin off my nose. Do go on with this talk. It's getting late."

Jimoh hated being hurried and as a sign of his displeasure, threw the half-smoked cigar on the rug and crushed it beneath his shoes. He met his host's glare with a disconcerting stare for some nerve-racking moments. The silence in the room was so complete that one could hear the drop of a pin. Finally Buko's eyes gave ground.

Jimoh resumed his baiting. "As I was saying, my company is still expanding. But this expansion is being hampered by the cut-throat competition in this sector of the economy. The more established ones are giving us much trouble. If we've got to leap in this expansion programme, then we got to have a fleet of more buses — ten can do. You're planning to marry in a month's time I suppose?"

Buko grinned proudly. "Words sure get around. The marriage ceremony is going to be a hit. When I start something, it's something."

"Sure, you're planning something super." A cunning smile flitted across Jimoh's face. "But you're going to have financial troubles, aren't you?"

Buko's chocolate-brown body turned darker and his eyes hardened. "Look mister, if you know what is good for you better finish the business you've come for. Don't start prying into my financial affairs. I have enough bread to last me a lifetime."

Jimoh had touched a delicate spot and he knew it. In fact it was done deliberately. He had handled men like Buko before and knew how to needle them without passing the limit. Buko's unease made his smile broaden.

"Don't burst on artery." He said. "As you said, words sure get around. I picked it up somewhere and it's spreading fast — that after this marriage you wouldn't have a dime in your pocket. I couldn't help listening to them. Those guys would need a lot of convincing that you've got enough bread to last you a lifetime."

"Let them think what they like." Buko's tone was beginning to soften. "None of these rumour-mongers will dare say such filth in my presence. If I'm going to listen anymore to your business plans, then you'd better get that thought out of your system. I'm content with the bread I have."

"How would you like to make five thousand naira?" Jimoh asked casually.

Five thousand! Buko's mouth turned dry suddenly. If he could get such an amount he wouldn't have to worry about this financial disaster he was heading for. By the time this money finished, he would have recovered from the extravagance of the forthcoming marriage ceremony. Nevertheless pride had made him so swollen-headed that he didn't want it to seem he was jumping at the opportunigy.

"Think I'm so poor or something?" He snapped at Jimoh in mock anger.

Jimoh got up and began to walk towards the door. "Well, forgive me. Didn't mean to hurt you. I thought you would be interested. So long." He turned the knob and opened the door.

"Okala!" Buko's voice, sharp and pleading, made the eunuch turn. "I .... I didn't mean to drive you away, Come let us ..... fin. . .ish the business." He stuttered in alarm. He had realised at the last moment that pride wouldn't get him anywhere with this man and the thought of the five thousand that was slipping through his fingers made him sick with his pride.

Jimoh paused, his hand on the door knob. He turned slowly and regarded his prey with pity. "You aren't poor. The bread you have can last you a life-time. So why worry about five thousand quid?"

"I'm not worrying. But if you haven't got anything doing with the money, I sure could do with it." He grinned lamely at Jimoh. "Don't mind me. I tend to get touchy sometimes. Come let's finish our business."

The repentant tone of his voice pleased Jimoh. It meant he wouldn't have much trouble any longer. He swaggered back to his chair and snake into it.

"You asked me whether I wanted to earn five thousand, didn't you? What am I going to do to earn it?"

"Nothing much. As I said before I want to purchase ten more buses. The Company doesn't have the money at present. What I want is for you to help me secure a loan from your bank."

"Why, that's not hard if you can provide evidence of collateral security. Our bank is one of the most liberal, as far as banks are concerned." He stared at Jimoh, his eyes suddenly alight with naked greed. "Bring the five thousand and the evidence tomorrow and I'll help you secure any amount you want."

Jimoh was gloating inwardly. Well here was it! His prey had swallowed the bait. If he handled him right the guy would swallow the line and sinker. How money can turn men into suckers!

"That's not all." He said thoughtfully as he prepared to dangle the line and sinker this time. "The five thousand would be yours tomorrow if you can assure me of swinging this loan thing. How would you like managing my business?"

Buko was flustered. "You joking or something?"

"Couldn't be more serious. Most of the guys working for me are numbskulls. I need someone as bright as you — someone who can handle them right. You're going to bring out the best in them." He paused to stare at the hooked prey. There was no escape this time. "The pay is twelve thousand a year, with some fringe benefits included. Come to my place tomorrow and we'll put finishing touches to this."

Buko was gaping at him. His heart hammered steadily and exciting bells jangled all over him. The thought of what 'Okala' had just said made his mouth dry. What a break! Twelve thousand! He wouldn't need to take any more orders from that creep of a Financial Manager. With a salary of twelve thousand he could afford to live big.

When he succeeded finally in moistening his lips, he grinned at Jimoh. "I guess you know how to hook someone. When do I see you tomorrow for the finishing touch?"

Jimoh glanced at his watch. "9.00 p.m. tomorrow I won't get back to my apartment in time and there's nothing like discussing business at home. The address is 4B Woods Avenue. Memorize it. You can't miss it once you reach Woods Avenue." He got up. "Guess I'll be leaving."

Buko accompanied him to the door. There Jimoh stopped to grin at him. "You know, once in a while a guy's got to boast to his friends. I'm not stopping you from telling people you're coming into big money. But don't tell anyone that you're getting it in order to secure a loan. Better still you don't mention me at all or even the loan until we've met tomorrow. It's good we're agreed before word spreads around." Still grinning he shook hands with Buko. "Your fiancee's got what it takes to turn a man on. When she's present a man can swallow a bee or he can be hugely generous just to impress her. Be seeing you."

Buko waited for a second, listening to his footfalls on the stairs then he closed the door and locked it. Going over to his table, he drew out a sheet of paper and wrote: Charles Okala, 4B Woods Avenue.

B

Siren screaming, Omo Baba brought the squad car to a screeching halt behind the ambulance. Getting out from the car, he began to swagger to where a group of Policemen were discussing. The disdain on his face was so apparent that most of the men stopped chattering as he approached.

Sergeant Phil Jumbo came out to meet him.

"The Chief arrived yet?" Omo Baba asked.

"No. Just the ambulance. Doctor Moziah and his men."

Nodding, Baba walked over to where medical attendants were clustered and sought out Doctor John Moziah, a middle-aged man with a fat face and eyes hardened from years of working in the Police force.

Seeing Baba walking towards him, his fat face split into a grin.

"I knew you would be here soon. How's the going?" He had a deep pleasant voice that didn't go with the hard eyes.

"Not bad. Heard a guy got knocked off. Where's the body?"

"Over there." Moziah said, pointing to a sheet-covered form that was surrounded by low shrubs. "The Chief coming?"

"Yeah." He began to walk towards the inert sheet-covered form followed by Moziah. "He's going to demand our flesh if that dead guy is his friend."

Moziah stiffened, staring at him with large bulging eyes. "Half his brains are sticking out of his head. A sorry sight. Wouldn't want to be in his place for all the world. If the guy's his friend, am I happy I'm not in your shoes." A teasing gleam came into his eyes. "When the chief explodes, there is an explosion."

Baba halted, looking down at the inert form as he tried to summon up his courage to raise the sheet. It wasn't that he hadn't seen dead men before. On the contrary, he'd seen many dead men in the course of his work as a Police Detective. The trouble was that when ever he saw a dead man, he had to control the impulse to throw up. On two occasions his efforts hadn't been fruitful for he had retched. When you're a cop such a sight reminds you of what would happen one day. A day when a criminal or a demented man is going to spread your guts on the floor.

Finally he raised the sheet with an unsteady hand and what he saw made him stand still to steady himself and control the orgy that was rushing up his throat.

The eyes were open and staring with something akin to pain; lips bared in a toothy horrible grin. Tendrils of hair and brain that had merged to form a grisly mixture were being investigated by ants. The body had already begun to swell and a large red hole stood out on the forehead.

Baba placed the sheet back, spat out and regarded Moziah inquisitively. When he was able to moisten his lips he asked. "What can you make of it, John?"

Moziah shrugged resignedly. To him dead bodies were nothing. "Probably got killed by high calibre slugs. One went right through the head. It's likely the other is inside. Don't bet on this until I perform an autopsy on him. You can have a comprehensive report then. Think you can track down the killer?"

"Maybe. Maybe not. I'm not promising anything. This could be one of the few unsolved murders if proved to be murder. Why guys have to get themselves knocked off in lonely spots like this is what I don't know." He looked towards a fast approaching car. "Here comes the Chief."

Chief of Police, Inspector Gerry Ogunbor, heaved his bulk out of the car and bounded onto the sidewalk with an agility that made mockery of his size.

He was tall and fat, with a clean-shaven face and an aggressive jaw. Beer had spoilt his figure. His tall, lean frame was no more. His tummy now stuck out like an accusing football. His face had turned fat and soft with the good life and the only trace of the ruthlessly efficient cop he used to be was the aggressive jaw. For a man who had just touched fifty his speed was still commendable considering the disadvantage of being pot-bellied.

Omo Baba went foward to meet him.

"Good evening, Chief."

Ogunbor nodded curtly. Obviously he wasn't pleased at having his sleep disturbed. "Where's the body?"

"This way, Chief." Baba led him to where the sheet-covered form lay, then backed away a little as the Chief raised the sheet.

The transformation was instant! Ogunbor's face contorted for a long trying moment, pain and hurt mingled in his eyes. This was a terrible blow. He had to control the wave of nausea that was sweeping over him. When he finally mastered himself, he walked back quickly to his car with drooping shoulders. Baba followed slowly behind.

Once seated on the back seat of the car, his legs resting on the ground, Ogunbor beckoned to all and sundry.

"The medical attendants can now go and carry the body." He waited until all the medical attendants had gone then he addressed Moziah: "John, you're going to perform the autopsy this night. Make a comprehensive report and deliver it to me personally. I am going to be personally involved in this case. The dead man was one of my best friends." He paused and continued in a subdued voice. "When a friend of mine gets knocked off, then it's an affront to me. So find something on that body that we're going to work on. Get all your men working on this immediately."

As Doctor Moziah hurried away, Ogunbor glared at the remaining men. Most of them didn't want to meet his eyes.

"This corpse you've just seen now was my friend. When any of my friends get killed, then someone is in for hell. His name's Tim Aina. Hear me? Tim Aina! He used to collect four thousand Naira from the bank every Thursday so that he could pay the guys working for him on Friday. Some of you probably know him — he's the proprietor of Omoregie Enterprises. It's my guess that someone who has been watching him for sometime knocked him off and made off with the money he was carrying. I have no doubt in my mind that this is murder — someone robbed and killed him." He stared hard at them trembling with a rage that made most of them shrink. They had never seen him in this mood before. "You're going to find his killer!" He spat out. "Turn this evil city upside down if possible but bring me his killer. I don't want any excuses. When someone murders my friend, I go after him. He'll run. He'll hide but I'll get him in the end. So you go get him! And none of you gets promoted until you come back with the killer. If any of you finds something — a clue, report to me personally. As I've said before I am in on this."

He dismissed them with a wave of the hand. Baba sidled over to the car and stood before the Chief. He was the Chief's favourite detective and knew that whatever the situation, the chief always relied on him to produce results. Usually he was given a private briefing from which he fed the others. Whenever there was a killing the whole case was put in his hands but this . . . .?

Noticing Baba standing before him, the Chief forced a grin but he was far from happy.

"You're playing a big part in this operation, Omo." The Chief told him. "You're going to conduct a separate investigation from the others but I'm going to be in charge of the whole operation. I want all reports and findings to me. If you bust this case I'll see you get a huge raise on your salary."

Baba nodded "Don't you think, Sir, that I'll need a free hand if I'm going to come up with something?"

"You've a free hand but I want all findings reported to me periodically. I've got to be in on this from start to finish." He stared intently at Baba. "You're starting now. I'm giving you the job of breaking it to the man's wife. Handle her gently but interrogate her. Not too hard. I'll see her later but not now. It's important she gets over the shock a little before I see her or we won't learn anything."

He gave baba her address then waved him off.

It took Baba a little over twenty minutes to drive to the house which was on the outskirts of town. As he steered his squad car into the drive lined with gravel that made crunching sounds under the tyres he sighed hugely. How the rich lived!

The house was a lonely marvellous piece of modern architecture with two garages and a patio that had creeping plants all over the walls. There was a lawn surrounded by trimmed Hibiscus, boys' quarters and small swimming pool with neon lights twinkling over it. He sucked in his breath, then approached the house and rang the bell.

The ringing of the bell sounded high and eerie in the silent night.

Dupe Aina opened the door herself and froze at the sight of the Policeman standing at the door.

"Detective Omo Baba. City Police." He flashed his identity card at her. "The Chief of police, Jerry Ogunbor, said I should call on you."

At the mention of Ogunbor's name her heart began beating again but she was still scared and shaking. "Come in. Come in." She said moving back into the sitting room to be followed by Baba. There was a tremor in her voice as she spoke. What was the meaning of this night call by the Police? Had something bad happened to Tim? Or had he done something silly? Many possibilities came flooding her mind and dropping away unanswered.

Omo Baba selected an easy chair in the room and sat down, fiddling with his identity card to hide the disgust on his face. What an immensely fat woman! She looked as though she was pregnant with a giant. Moreover Baba was feeling his way around, looking for a way to begin before breaking the news. The deep tremor in her voice had rattled him. If there was still some love left between this blubber of fat and her husband, then the world was going to pieces. What for Pete's sake would a man still find amusing in this bloated body?

"You said Ogunbor sent you." The woman's voice interrupted his thoughts. "Has it to do with my husband? Anything the trouble?"

Baba cleared his throat. "Well, yes." He said hesitantly, then hardened his resolve. He'd better spill the beans to the woman if he wasn't going to stay here all night. "It's got to do with your husband. He — he's dead."

The look of raw pain in her eyes jolted him. The glass of whisky she had hitherto been holding but which he hadn't noticed slipped out of her fingers and fell on the rug, the liquid sloshing over her ankles.

She closed her small eyes and for a moment he thought she was going to faint. But she was a courageous woman, no doubt. After that agonising moment she recollected herself and looked at him, tears in her eyes.

"Tell me what . . . . what happened. How did he die? What killed him?"

"He was murdered, madam."

"Murdered?" Her voice was a horrified croak. "Who murdered him? What did Tim do to warrant his being killed?"

"Well madam that's why I'm here. We haven't got a clue as to who murdered him. But we have a theory as to why he could have been killed. He . . . ."

"Why was he killed?" She asked, involuntarily going to sit down on a chair.

"You probably know that he goes to collect money from the bank every Thursday. Ogunbor said the money's to the tune of four thousand.

When we found him there wasn't a kobo on him. It's our opinion that whoever killed him made away with the money. He was probably killed for the money."

"You're going to find his murderer?" She slanted her eye brows hopefully.

"It depends." He said evasively. "If he was killed by commonplace armed robbers then it would be difficult to nail them unless I get a lucky break. If he was killed by someone he knows, then maybe nailing the guy wouldn't be so difficult. Nevertheless to track down the killer I'm going to need all the help I can get from you. Think you would be able to answer a few questions?"

She was about to nod in the affirmative when some words flirted through her mind. "Your husband is possibly in some woman's arms now, probably a whore, imagine competing with a whore . . . ."

The momory of those harsh words was like a blow on the solar plexus. Where was Tim when he died? She suddenly realized that she hadn't cried when this detective announced to her the death of her husband. Though she had experienced a genuine stab of pain and shock — plus a few tears that hadn't flowed down, she now realized that those words had been lurking in her subconscious and had influenced her emotional reaction when she learnt of Tim's death.

"Where did you find my husband's body?" Her voice sounded husky.

Looking thoughtfully at her, Baba realized what was going on inside her mind. He made a mental note of that. "At Junction 15.

Near the Highway to Lagos. He was lying near some shrubs by the roadside with his brains hanging out. Shot from close range." He watched her carefully as he spoke, then glanced at his watch. "I have a few questions to ask madam."

"Go on." She prodded this time.

He brought out a notebook, proceeded to scribble something on it, then asked: "Your name please?"

"Mrs. Dupe Aina."

"Address?"

Her small eyes hardened into pinpoints. "How do you happen to be here if you didn't know the address?"

"Mere formality, madam." He said respectfully though his fingers were trembling with rage.

"4 Wombie Lane."

"How many years have you been married to Mr. Aina?"

"Seventeen years."

"Any kids?"

"Three."

"You guys been living happily all these years?"

"Who do you think you are?" Her voice was sharp. "I won't have you prying into my private affairs."

Omo Baba controlled his temper with an effort. The fat bitch! He thought. She was an utter disgrace to feminity. "Well madam, when a murder is committed, police investigators pry into the private life of the deceased. The motive for the murder of a person usually lies in his or her private life." He gave her a grin. "Maybe you could oblige to . . . ."

"Okay, if it means anything to you we've been living happily all along." She avoided his eyes as she spoke, picking up the fallen glass of whisky in the process.

Her shifty eyes told Baba she was lying or wasn't telling the truth entirely. "You lived happily up till today?" He needled gently, knowing that this was a sensitive ground to most women.

"I told you before." She replied. "Though there are small frictions now and then, sometimes a little quarrel but generally we are a happy couple."

"When did you have the last quarrel or friction if I may ask?"

"What on earth are you suggesting?" Her tone had taken on the sharp edge.

"I mean when you people had the last quarrel?"

She sighed resignedly. "If you must know there has been some friction between us since this working week began. Why do you ask?"

'Here comes the moment' Baba thought. He was going to deflate this bloated bitch. How he would like to see the wind go out of her.

"If there was some trouble, it could have upset him. It's possible he could have found someone — some woman to make him forget. Mind you, this is a theory but it just could be possible. A man who thinks there's no peace at home can go and find peace with some other woman. If he was with a woman when he died, then it's possible she could have been involved one way or the other in his death."

Dupe closed her eyes and bit hard on her lips until she drew blood. She fought an internal battle to contain her smouldering anger. For a moment Baba thought he'd opened his mouth too loud as he saw her fingers tighten on the glass she was holding. Then he relaxed with an inner grin as she sighed deeply.

"Watch your tongue, young man. If you don't want your arse in the fire, then be careful when speaking to me." Try as much as she did to make her voice forceful, there was no camouflaging the subdued note in it.

Baba shrugged. "I didn't mean to hurt you." He lied cheerfully. "Do you think your husband had any enemies?"

"Can't say. He was a harmless man. Had a lot of friends. But enemies? There are enemies even among friends."

"Try to think. He could have mentioned sometime about having a quarrel with someone at the office. Someone who knows he collects four thousand from the bank every Thursday."

Her face screwed up thoughtfully as she rummaged inside her mind. At last she said. "Can't remember now. I'll think about it later."

A little boy of around six came out from one of the bedrooms. Wearing pyjamas he walked barefooted to where his mother was.

"That your kid?" Baba asked unnecessarily.

"Mummie, is dad not back yet?" The kid asked, climbing onto his mother's laps.

She had been so preoccupied with the policeman's questions that she hadn't had time to reason properly. With a shock she realized that her children were now fatherless. Putting her face in her palms she began to wail.

Baba looked at her pitifully. He was quick to understand why she had suddenly burst out wailing. Knowing he couldn't get anything more from her for the meantime he got up, patted the kid on the back and walked out of the room.

IV

A

Gilt Jimoh fingered his passionless piece of manhood without any feeling of self-pity. He had stopped wallowing in useless self-pity sometime ago. All his mental and physical energy was now geared towards criminal activities — to humiliate the society that had made him impotent. If some guys happened to die in the process, too bad. On the other hand if he happened to grow rich, then it was an added feather to his growing criminal stature.

He yawned, then sat up in bed and glanced at the bedside clock. 7.00 a.m. He pulled out a drawer and rummaged inside for his shaving kit. His spirits were high this morning. Maybe it was the knowledge that if all went well today by midnight, his gang would be millions of Naira rich. He had pulled many jobs in his time but never a job of this magnitude — a job that required painstaking plans to ensure that all went well. This would probably be his last big job, but he was going to continue humiliating the society that had turned him into an "impotent".

Inevitably his mind went back to that eventful day when fate was to turn a harsh hand on him. He could remember the ugly lady-doctor who had hairs on her chest and muscles like a street brawler. Of course he had only pretended to love her. All those tiresome nights he had spent making love to her just because of her money had become too much for him. The ugly insatiable wench! She had taught him one technique after another — the hydra-stroke, the dog-stroke, the plunger. No man could withstand such rigours — albeit with that ugly wench. He had cracked on the tenth day.

After one of those jarring early-morning sessions, she had left for work. Fatigued to the marrow and utterly disgusted, he had staggered to the liquor cabinet and downed a bottle of whisky. Of course he must have been dead drunk to have risked taking the doctor's maid in her room. Though the maid had provided the relief he needed from the doctor's violent love making, she had caught them red-handed. She had apparently forgotten something and came back to collect it. The door had been open and she'd walked in on them. What ensued later was foggy to him — he would only add guess work to likely facts. . . . .

A syringe — something like a hypodermic syringe — had plunged into his body and before he knew it, he had blacked out. When he woke up he had felt very weak, his mind fuddled and a slight pain throbbing in his scrotal sack. Instinctively, his hand had gone to his scrotum and to his horrified indignation his balls weren't there any more. He had felt around in desperation to make sure — but, sure, they weren't there. Shaking, he had got up slowly from the bed and glanced around. And there was the lady-doctor sitting at the bedside table grinning at him. With his balls in her palm!

She'd probably operated on him while he was out and extracted his testes. The hate in her eyes as she grinned at him had chilled him to the marrow. Weak and almost spineless from the effects of the drug she had given him, he had climbed down from the bed.

"How are you feeling, Gilt?" She had asked, rolling the delicate balls in her palm.

"What's this? What's the meaning of this, Joan? Joan!. . . . ."

With bulging eyes he had watched her throw the balls into her mouth like they were tablets. Then with a sinking feeling — a feeling that gave way to an exploding rage he watched her chew the balls in relish and wash the particles down with whisky.

He'd exploded all right. Weak and nerveless as he had been, it was later he realized the strength rage can give one. Diving at the mirrow on the table he had brought it crashing down on her head and proceeded to carve her to pieces. He went demented, his mind ripped into tatters. That had been his first killing and he'd buried her in the garden. The maid had simply vanished into thin air, he hadn't seen her again. His guess was that the doctor had murdered her. At that time he'd feared he would die from the operation but somehow he survived. But only just.

Jimoh came out of his reverie and found to his annoyance that he was gripping his shaving kit fiercely. From then he had developed a destructive complex that had reached startling proportions. His main purpose in life now was to live and destroy. He hated women now — especially hairy women. Now and then when he saw a hairy broad and he was in the mood, he lured her into a secluded place and slashed off her breasts. He would put the 'meat' in the fire and when they started spluttering, he would feed them to a friendly dog that lived next door.

In fact Jimoh had started making plans about how to spend his cut of tonight's steal. Once he laid his hands on the bread, he was going to have himself one big bang of fun. He would move into a big flat, buy a Mercedes Benz car and find a homosexual. He would buy some huge wolf hounds and on the night of every new moon get some girls' breasts for the wolf hounds. He would . . . .

His half-crazy, destruction-obsessed mind reeled as a continuous stream of schemes rolled through them. Getting up lazily, he went to the bathroom to shave.

It took him forty-five minutes to bathe, dress and rush through a breakfast. Fifteen minutes later he was at Kpondo's down-the-mill shack, seated at a table and staring at the expectant faces gathered round the table.

"We're going over the plans of yesterday." He began briskly, an animated light in his eyes. "You guys ready?"

"Everyone's here except that cursed Bank Manager." Joe Puna stated, regarding Jimoh with slightly hooded eyes. "Aren't we going to wait for him?"

"There's no need for him to be seen around with us in broad daylight. It could be risky once we rob that bank; there's nothing about this operation he doesn't have at his finger-tips. Two of us have gone over the plan several times before. For the benefit of you guys we'll go over the plan again." He looked slowly around the table, noting the expression on each face. His eyes met Furo Kpondo's and stopped. He stared fixedly at him for some time.

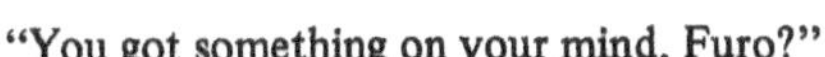

"You got something on your mind, Furo?"

Kpondo nodded. "I'm scared. Had a bad dream last night. Don't think I can go along with this operation anymore."

"Dream or no dream you're sticking with us. I said last night that anybody who wanted to quit had better quit before I laid down the plans. Now there's no quitting. Try to quit and you're living on borrowed time."

Kpondo pondered over this. Finally. "so I'm not quitting. I'll have to consult a fortune-teller after this meeting. He could interpret the dream for me."

"What in hell's name do you want to consult a fortune-teller for?" Young demanded. "Over a mere dream? You turning soft or something?"

"Suppose he narrates the dream first?" Puna put in quietly. "Never condemn a man when you haven't heard what he's got to say."

Jimoh stared at him, his face a study in rage. "Either way, no one is quitting. All of us are in this now and there's no backing out."

"The dream first." Puna repeated.

Kpondo licked his lips nervously. Sweat poodles were beginning to form on his sagging face.

"I was sleeping when I dreamt I was in a graveyard, dressed in a black outfit. Then there was a rumbling sound and one of the graves opened. Jimoh came out of the grave and began to advance towards me. He was swathed in bandages from head to foot. In his hands were some money .... probably naira bills. As I stepped back ready to run, my left foot hit a coffin behind me and it split in two. There was a ghostly noise from inside the coffin, then the sides came totally apart and Ify stepped out of the coffin. I ...."

"Stop that crap! Ify shrieked, covering her ears to prevent herself from hearing more. "We're going along with the operation! No backing out!"

Kpondo stared at the others with a fixed, triumphant grin. "Do I go on?"

Jimoh, watching the reactions on their faces, noted that Young and Ify were visibly shaken. Puna's face was a fathomless mask. He realized now that to have allowed Kpondo to narrate the dream was

50

a mistake. It had sown the seeds of fear among the members of his gang. He spoke.

"Enough of that trash, Furo. As I said before, no one is backing out." He paused then continued. "I don't believe in fortune-tellers. They're all dupes and fakes. No one is consulting any fortune-tellers. Last night we all agreed to go through with this operation. Any guy that tries to veer away from that line is living on borrowed time."

"No backing out, eh?" Kpondo queried, a sickening feeling inside his stomach.

"Look mister, when I say no quitting, I mean no quitting. I'm trying to make all of us rich and what do I get? Guys trying to quit at the last minute." He stared at Kpondo disconcertingly. "You're an old man, Furo. Got maybe a few days, a few months or years to live on earth. You've got little to lose. If you want to live your last days on earth in paradise, if you want to be rich and enjoy the power of money — young girls, fun, a nice house, a Mercedes Benz car, if you want to live the easy way, then there's no easier road, mister."

"If you also want to head for destruction, there's no easier road." Kpondo added calmly.

Jimoh managed to keep his temper in check. "As agreed last night, Bill goes to befriend that cop woman today. How he does it is his own business. When she has finished preparing the food for those guards at the bank, Bill lures her into the bedroom with promises ..... probably more love-making. Before then he must have made sure that the kitchen door or window is open. While he is entertaining the woman, Ify enters and dopes the food. The drug is enough to knock out a mule and take effect after two hours because of the delayed action. When the cop woman returns from the bank, Bill knocks her off to sew up that end."

His sharp eyes went round the table balefully as he paused to wipe a dribble of saliva from the corner of his mouth.

"This is where you take over Joe. As I said yesterday, once we rob this bank the lousy cops in this city are going to know there was inside help. No one can pull such a neat job on a heavily guarded bank like that without inside help .... no, not one. What this means is that we'll have to get a fall guy. And there's no guy better suited for this than one Mike Buko, an Assistant Manager in the bank. I've arranged with him to come to our new apartment along Woods Avenue at 9.00 p.m. tonight. He'll be coming along with his fiancee. Joe, it's your job and Ify's to knock off the pair of them. No guns, mind you. We don't want to attract attention. After killing them, you dump them in one of the rooms and join up with us near the bank. You musn't make a mistake in this part of the operation or our friend Obi would lose his nerve. If he loses his nerve, something might go wrong during the robbery; even if the robbery is unsuccessful he could crack under police interrogation."

Joe Puna grinned at him. "If he loses his nerve, too bad. I wouldn't mind killing him the way you swat a fly."

"I'm running this gang, not you." Jimoh said crisply, a warning edge to his voice. "What I say goes. You don't knock a guy off until I say so. We may eventually have to button Obi's mouth but why not wait until he loses his nerve."

"Seems we're taking too much trouble to cover our tracks." Puna said grudgingly. "When a guy covers his tracks too well that's when he gets nabbed."

Jimoh ignored him. "The third part of the operation, which is robbing the bank comes into being after ten .... possibly around ten-twenty tonight. I've said it before and I'll say it again; Obi is handling this part of the operation. He's got the keys into the bank and its vault. No one touches anything until he says so. We don't want to trigger off any alarms."

"Wait a minute!" Ify said sharply. "There's a flaw here. There're twenty-four guards, Okay? If by chance one or two of them don't take the food, there could be trouble."

Jimoh smiled his false, slippery smile. He liked having smart guys around him, guys who can ask only smart questions or make smart remarks. In fact, he was prepared for this flaw.

He said, "Leave this area to me. If any of them is not asleep when the robbery is due, I'll take care of him. Assuming all goes well, the last part of the operation is the get-away. You guys know the curfew starts at ten. There's a road block near the bank and all cars going in and out are checked. Just when the robbery is taking place, Kpondo steals an ambulance vehicle. Dressed as ambulance attendants, we'll get easy passage at the road block. Once past the road block, we'll drive straight to our new apartment. We'll split the money next tomorrow when the initial heat must have cooled slightly. I don't have to remind you guys not to start a spending spree immediately after the split. A nosey cop could just decide to find who you are and where you got all that money. Once a cop latches unto you in this city, you're a goner. So after the bread has been shared, we'll all have to be content with living on that four thousand for a few days more. When movement in and out of the city becomes easier, everyone splits and goes his separate way. Bill can go have himself a ball on the moon; Ify can buy new shoes . . . ."

Ify sucked in her breath and released it in a huge shudder. Two hundred and fifty thousand naira! She could never have believed there was all that much bread in the world. With that kind of money she would surely do more than buy new shoes. She would leave here for Lagos. Once there she'd rent a marvellous flat, buy a Ford Mustang and spend endless hours lazing about on the beach and taking the best young men who came her way. Marriage wasn't for her. She wouldn't want to get tied to a dreary home . . . . to some dreary suckling and noisy children who would always be fighting among themselves. That would be sheer boredom. She was going to live her whole life on the beach, get back all those years of fun she had missed. It was going to be one big bang of a ball.

"Any need to carry guns along tonight?" Young, who had been silent for most of the morning, asked.

"Of course." Jimoh replied.

"Why? Guns could be risky if we're going to pass a road block."

"Don't be a dope." Jimoh said impatiently. "Of course it could be risky but we're going to take the risk. I've tried to drum into you guys one thing, we're not expecting trouble; but if by chance trouble starts and there is no way out then I'm starting a gun play. Anybody who thinks he can stop me robbing that bank had better take a dive into hell. If he tries, too bad. I'll blast a gaping hole in his guts."

He yawned and got up from the table. "Furo, I see you've disposed of that Range Rover. You're becoming smart. Saved me the trouble of having to tell you." He walked to the door, turned the knob. "So Bill you start the ball rolling by befriending that cop woman. See me later for her address. Any mistake and your balls wouldn't be worth much to you after that." He banged the door behind him and went out.

Looking at Young, Kpondo suddenly began to laugh. He laughed for a very long time that even after the laughter subsided, its ringing continued in the confines of the room.

B

The sun came down mercilessly in shimmering rays, making the air hot and stuffy. The time was a little past noon — not normally the hottest time of day. But today, even at this time of day the temperature was so high that for the superstitious there was only one possible explanation for it — the sun-god was angry.

Omo Baba trudged on in the hot sunshine, ignoring the hostile glances from some people. Fatigue was beginning to show in his walk, in his usual swagger. He didn't swagger now but dragged himself along. For a sizeable part of the morning he had been digging, cajoling, trying to find a lead to the murder of Tim Aina. He had merely come up against a blank wall. Most of the people he had questioned didn't know anything or pretended not to know. Furious, he had been about to call it quits for the day when a message came through to him that the Range Rover had been found abandoned.

This new development had boosted his sagging morale considerably. In higher spirits he had raced over to where the car was found and come up against a more exasperating blank wall. No finger prints. The whole car had been dusted of finger prints. No one seemed to know how the Rover came to be there. One fool was even positive the Rover had been there for a week. Tired and more infuriated than before, he had left the scene and began to walk towards the house of a fortune-teller.

After many years in his work, Baba had come to realise that failure breeds fatigue and anger. Whenever he felt a sense of failure about a case, the investigations easily made him tired and he flew into a rage at the slightest provocation.

He paused in front of the mud-walled, ramshackle house that was thatched with leaves. The door was of rotten wood and termites were busy chewing away at it. A pleasant aroma of cooking was coming from inside the house. He hesitated a moment, undecided, then knocked on the door reluctantly.

"Come in."

The door creaked sharply as he entered the dark, almost airless room.

"Welcome, my son Omo Baba." The ageing fortune-teller said. "I've been expecting you." He was sitting on a worn-out mat.

"How come, you know my name? Baba asked, impressed.

"My job is to know who is coming, son. I communicate with the spirit world-with our fore-fathers. They tell me who is coming and what he comes for."

"And what have I come for?" Baba was a trifle rattled. Though he had always heard of the capabilities of fortune-tellers his attitude towards their powers had been skeptical.

"You had a dream which you want interpreted. The dream is true — this city is about to explode any minute."

Baba stiffened. "What do you mean?" The fortune-teller shook out some cowries from a bag beside him. Using a long piece of chalk he wrote some things on the floor, things which didn't make any meaning to Baba. Then he rolled one of the cowries across the floor. He watched it settle, his lips moving unintelligibly. He rolled another cowrie after the first and missed it.

"Evil spirits!" He spat out. "A lot of evil spirits roaming about."

He rolled two more cowries after the first. The last hit it. "Evil spirits." He muttered again and began meditating. He meditated for around three minutes and when he finished, he wrote more things on the floor. Using his local fan made of palm fronds, he began fanning himself in the act of driving away evil spirits. When he finally looked up he was frowning.

"Police life is bad, you know?"

"What's that?" Baba asked sharply. "I didn't come for an analysis of my work."

The fortune-teller shook his head sadly. "I just saw a castrated bull and lots of money."

"Meaning what?" There was a tinge of impatience in the younger man's voice now.

A shrug. "You have a potential enemy. Your forefathers were willing to show me the enemy and the trouble he is going to give you. But his forefathers blurred my view into the spirit land and all I could see was a castrated bull and lots of naira bills."

"What for madness sake is all this about a castrated bull and lots of money?" Baba's voice had shot up a note. "Has this got anything to do with the coming explosion of the city? Can't you find out?"

Even in the darkened room Baba could make out the greed in the old man's eyes as he shook his head.

"Sure, it has got something to do with the coming explosion. But I can't find out the meaning. Anyway not for now." He paused, that greedy glint in his eyes. "A fortune-teller once in a while needs protection from the evil forces he is battling against. Before I inquire further about this case we've got to offer a sacrifice to the gods. We've got to protect ourselves and bring the neutral spirits to the side of your forefathers."

"What are we going to need for the sacrifice?"

"Two white cocks. Two eggs from a goose. Two large kola nuts and a head of tobacco. My personal fee is four naira. Until then I can't do anything. Needless to remind you that your life could be in danger."

"What makes you think my life could be in danger?"

"Nothing. Just a hunch. You're a policeman, aren't you? In your work you come across all sorts of people, make enemies easily. In the meantime beware of eunuchs. If you come across any eunuch, better be careful how you handle him." He stared at Baba for some time in the gloom. "Don't try to tackle him until we've performed the sacrifice." He added as an afterthought.

Baba felt anger tightening in his chest. He had always heard that fortune-tellers were cheats, dupes and cut-throats. He didn't know whether he could trust this one. There was something soft and smooth about this man which he was beginning to dislike. It was no secret that many fortune-tellers used some of the items they had requested for sacrifice for their own personal meals.

"You mean if any eunuch guy starts any gun play with me, I should back out? Take to my heels?"

"I mean you should avoid trouble as best as you can especially if a eunuch is involved. Any trouble and there's a eunuch around, you get away from there as fast as possible. If you can get the items and fee ready by tomorrow, then you'll need avoid a eunuch only for today."

"Nothing more?"

"Two white cocks. Two goose eggs. Two large kola nuts. A head of tobacco plus four naira."

"Go rot in hell, you cut-throat!"

"What? Amadioha the god of thunder . . . ." The fortune-teller began incredulously, then seeing Baba walking towards the door, he sprang up. "My fee, you son of the devil . . . .!"

"Go not in hell!" Baba snarled and banged the door behind him.

$$V$$

$$A$$

Bill Young lay on the cabinet-bed, watching a wall-gecko stalk a fly. It pleased him to see how the wall-gecko approached carefully, how its victim didn't realise, until the last moment, the fatal danger which it was in. And when it realised, it was too late! The fly only realised it in its death throes as the gecko's mouth closed over it.

He was the wall-gecko. Bisi Eyo was the fly. Thinking over it, now he realised how easy it had been to befriend Bisi Eyo, the cop-woman.

He had waited in a dark alley opposite her house, watching the approach to the house for thirty minutes. The waiting had begun to bore him, making him impatient. Then when he was about to let out a vile curse, she had quickly appeared, walking towards the house in a hurry. He had leapt out of his hiding place and with quick but casual steps had approached her.

She was ugly! How utterly ugly! The sight of her had left him with a deep resentment for Jimoh. Swallowing his revulsion he had flashed a forced smile at her. His smile alone had seemed to jolt her and he sensed her head reeling. Calling her 'fine lady', he'd told her he was new to the city, he wanted to know where the Police Station was and that he'd been wandering when he saw her.

She had started to give him directions to the station when he demanded for a glass of water to cool his tongue. Inside the house, he'd told her what a lovely policewoman she was, introduced himself falsely and . . . .

How easy it had been! Her long suffering eyes and body had brought out in him something unusual. Pity. Within twenty minutes they were in bed. Her insatiable demands had drained him and for a long time after he stopped, she'd kept moving her hips in anticipation of more. How she'd moaned and clawed him. The ugly bitch had been a virgin before he screwed her.

He sighed. The dangers of bottled-up love! Hers had been bottled up for too long. He regarded the scratches on his body. They were testimonies of their explosive love-making. After, she had left him explaining she had to go to the kitchen to prepare some supper. She finished preparing the food around 7 p.m. Leaving one of the kitchen windows open, he had steered her into the bedroom for more love-making. Their orgasm had been a shattering climax. They had exploded together — again and again. During the explosions, someone had tripped over something in the kitchen — probably Ify. He had heard it. But her sex-crazed senses had refused to function. Knowing that Ify would be doping the food then, he had concentrated his energy in a final, gurgling release that had left her gasping and sobbing for more.

A police Land-Rover had arrived then and she'd hurried out to tell the driver she was coming. When she was leaving for the bank with the food, she'd told him to wait for her — that she would be back around 8.30. He glanced at his watch, now 8.15. He had only fifteen minutes left.

Reluctantly he got up from the bed and began to search for a weapon. He hated having to kill her. Inwardly he knew he wouldn't be trying to go through with this under other circumstances — not even for two hundred and fifty thousand. In fact he would gladly have forgotten his share of the coming take if only to be relieved of the mental torture of having to murder her. This was the first time emotional consideration was creeping into his criminal operation. Not that he felt anything like love for her. She was too revolting to be his style. Even at the beginning when they were trying to start the love-making she hadn't aroused him. He had had to grit his teeth to force an erection. He pitied her — her sex-starved body and the torture she had gone through. This was the birthright of every woman — to be greased once in a while. He had been proud of the happiness he'd given her but now he was going to have to kill her. No, he couldn't do this. He must be mad to be thinking of murdering her, he told himself.

'Any mistake and your balls wouldn't be worth much to you after that.'

Jimoh's harsh words cut into him like a knife through butter. He didn't doubt the eunuch when he said that. That impotent lump could kill him without batting an eyelid. Knowing the eunuch, he recognised the fact that the guy wouldn't kill him immediately. He would probably remove his balls first . . . .

No, he musn't think of this. He had to kill Bisi Eyo. His personal survival ranked above hers. He would be sorry for it. It was going to give him nightmares but he had to go through with it. In his mind's eye he could see mutilated corpse of the girl he had raped and killed when he was seventeen. He pushed it away from his mind quickly. Glancing at his watch he realized he had little time left. It was 8.23.

On the bedside table was a knife. In the dim light of the room the knife glistened. He discarded the knife. It would be too messy. Under the bed was a hockey stick. He picked it up and felt the edges in his palm. Yes. This was the ideal weapon. He would deal her one fatal blow with the hockey stick that she wouldn't have time to scream. His heart was beating dully as he weighed the hockey stick in his hands. It was strong enough to crack a woman's skull with one blow. To his irritation he noticed that his hands were shaking slightly and sweat was running down his forehead.

He tried to steady his hands, telling himself he would be helping her out by killing her. She was damn too ugly to get any real happiness out of this wicked world. Anyway, even if he didn't knock her off Jimoh would finish her off too.

"Tony!"

He almost dropped the hockey stick. The sound of her voice had startled him. He hadn't known she was at the window watching him. How long had she been there? Did she suspect what he was planning to do?

He glanced at the window. He could only make out the outline of her head for it was dark outside — lowering his eyes he called out quickly. "So you've come back, Bisi. Quick of you, isn't it?"

"Tony, I have a feeling someone entered my kitchen. That person tripped over the container of water I keep near the window kitchen."

A big stream of sweat ran down his forehead and settled near his eyes.

"No one entered that kitchen all this time. Stop being suspicious. You coming in or not?"

"No Tony! I'm positive about it!" Her tone was sharp and frightened. "Something funny is happening here. I've a feeling someone is trying to do me in."

"Oh, stop making me nervy." He tried to keep his voice soft but found it was going up. "I threw away the water in that container. Didn't mean to scare you but mosquitoes breed in such water." He paused then added foolishly. "But I didn't enter that kitchen."

"There are footsteps on the window frame. Someone is in that kitchen."Go and check Tony. I'm scared."

"Okay, so I entered the kitchen. I was hungry. After throwing away the water in that container, I decided to climb through the window as it was quicker. You didn't leave me any food."

"You're lying, Tony! You weren't the person who entered that kitchen. There's more to this than meets the eye."

Though a cop she still could scare easily like most women.

"You tired of screwing?" He glanced up as he tossed the bait at her.

"No, I'm not tired." She replied quickly. "But . . . . Tony, stop looking at me in that way!" Her voice had reached the peak of panic.

"Oh bullshit. You're beginning to shout."

"Go and investigate the kitchen. Someone could be lying in wait there. I was murdered in a dream last night. One man, I couldn't see his face, cracked my skull open with a hockey stick."

"You're talking nonsense. No one is touching you as far as I'm here. Stay there while I investigate the kitchen."

His heart was banging violently as he crouched and began advancing towards the kitchen door. He was thinking to himself that if she saw the hockey stick she might get ideas. Maybe his luck was holding so far. He was going to jump through the kitchen window and come upon her from the back of the house.

"Tony! You're carrying a hockey stick!"

"I'm going to investigate the kitchen." He moved quickly into the kitchen, kicked a pot deliberately and climbed onto the window leading to the back of the house. He circled the house and paused at the corner, nearest the bedroom window where she was standing. He balanced the hockey stick expertly in his hands and cocked his ears to one side, listening for a long trying moment. Hearing nothing except the dull kicking of his heart against its pericardial sac, he came out of the corner and began to advance towards her on tiptoes. He moved on the balls of his feet making as little noise as possible.

Five steps more . . . . four . . . . tree . . . . two.

She must have sensed the presence of another being near her for she turned at the last moment. The look of abject terror mixed with surprise in her eyes chilled him to the bone and made him hesitate a moment, the hockey poised in the air. Then she was off, running and screaming before he could react. Seeing her running galvanised him into action. He sprang after her.

Terror made her run fast and blindly. Instead of running for the road she ran for the alley, screaming shrilly. He came after her, naked and furious. It was dark inside the alley and he couldn't make her out but just followed her footsteps. He was gaining fast on her, running with all his strength and knowing he had to stop her before the neighbours came to investigate. She tripped over a stone and stumbled. Coming at full speed behind her he didn't react fast enough and tripped over her. He rolled over, scrambled up quickly and caught one of her legs as she tried to spring away again. He spun her to the ground and dived on top of her.

"No, Tony no." She whimpered desperately, her hands going up involuntarily to protect her face.

"Sorry baby. Sorry. I have to do this." He said in between breaths, his chest heaving and sweat pouring from his armpit. Then his hands closed over her throat, shutting out air to her wind-pipe.

She fought him violently, scratching, kicking and biting. He held her down with his weight, his heart beating rapidly and sweat running into his eyes. He wasn't sure how it happened but suddenly her right hand came free and she jabbed her fingers into his eyes. He howled in pain as she threw him off her with all her strength. Trying to sit up, his hands closed over the hockey stick. He could hear her quick breathing as she prepared to run again. He swung the hockey stick with all the strength he could muster and heard the distinct breaking of her legs. Her sorrowful yelp of pain was cut off as he slammed the hockey stick, this time against her skull and felt brain and blood splash all over his body.

Feeling sick and ready to throw up, Young wiped the fingerprints on her throat with her dress. He knew she was dead. No one could survive that blow. Still using her dress he wiped prints off the hockey stick. He wasn't leaving any finger prints behind. He hadn't known all along he was still naked. It irritated him to discover that.

Suddenly he stiffened. There were footsteps and voices coming his way. He moved forward quickly, his heart thudding. Flattening himself against the wall of the alley, he held his breath. A torch flashed on near him and for a long sickening moment, he thought the game was up.

Three men passed very close to him. He waited for some time, then satisfied they were gone, he went back to the corpse. Holding one of the legs he dragged it to a large boulder in the alley. He squeezed it behind the boulder knowing it would take some time to discover the body.

Moving quickly, he sprinted out of the alley on his toes, paused a moment to make sure no one was watching him. Satisfied he walked quickly to the house, collected his things and paused to wipe prints off any item he must have touched. There was a loud knock on the door which startled him. Naked and carrying his clothes on his arm, he jumped through the back window and fled into the bush.

B

Joe Puna glanced at his watch. 8.59 p.m. He bagan fiddling with the piano wire in his hands. Jimoh had said that Mike Buko would be coming at 9.00. Trust the slick eunuch to always make elaborate plans and see to it that they are carried out. Jimoh had said he, Puna, was to fix Mike Buko while Ify took care of Buko's fiancee. But he was going to be alert in case Ify bungled hers. One thing he liked was the seclusion of their new apartment for no one was likely to hear a scream.

Reflecting on how Jimoh had baited Buko, Joe admitted the cleverness of the eunuch. He had explained to Joe how he had baited the Assistant Financial Manager of Bendel State Bank. A smart plan, Joe had agreed. But what he didn't quite agree to then was Jimoh's insistence that Pat Ola, Buko's financee would come along too. Joe had considered that assumption dangerous. Though Jimoh had said he hinted to Buko that Pat was a beautiful lady and with her around, a man might give him anything he wanted, Joe wasn't quite convinced that she would come. Admitted that if Buko thought the pressence of his financee might get him a better deal from 'Okala', he would surely bring her along. But Joe was slightly worried that the hint might have been lost on Buko despite the eunuch's assurances.

Joe hardly ever worried about the prospect of having to kill someone. He never shied away from the thought. This was probably due to the fact that he'd killed many times before. During the Nigerian civil war he'd knocked off a sizeable number of rebel soldiers. Therefore when he was dismissed from the army for some serious offence, he'd merely diverted his energies to criminal activities. In the course of his armed-robbery operations he'd had to silence some guys. He merely regarded that as a means of survival.

The sound of a car coming into the drive made him stiffen. He went over to the window, cautiously parted the curtain and peered outside. Sure there was a man and a woman getting out of the car — probably Buko and his fiancee. Trust the eunuch . . . .

Moving back, he walked quickly to the bedroom door and thrust his head inside.

"You'd better get ready Ify. The've arrived."

He fiddled with the piano wire some more, then thrust it into his pocket as the bell rang.

Putting on a fixed smile, he opened the door and stood aside.

"Mr. Okala in?" Buko asked, a little puzzled. He had been expecting a very large mansion with a swimming pool, big lawns, gilt-edged mirrors and deep easy chairs. Even the furniture in his apartment was better than these. He shrugged. He was always coming across men who swam in bread but didn't know what to do with all their money. Maybe this Okala was one of these squares.

"Yes sir." Puna replied, bowing to give the impression he was a servant. He led them inside. "Sit down, sir."

Puna shut the door as Buko and Pat sat down. He scratched his head a little servily.

"Who may I say has come, sir?"

"Mike. Mike Buko."

Puna bowed and pretended to make for the bedroom door. Once behind Buko he whipped out the piano wire, flung it over his victim's head unto the neck and strung it tight, choking back the scream that rose from the guy's throat.

Pat glanced beside her, saw what was happening and her hand went to her mouth. She rushed at Joe, hit him on the neck and started tugging at the hands that held the wire which was throttling her finance and her future. She screamed as she attacked. Ify who was just barging into the room, dragged her away to another corner of the room.

Joe held his victim down forcefully with all his strength as the guy's legs thrashed about desperately. His breathing was coming in laboured gasps. He could hardly control the life or death struggles of Buko, but he held on firmly, his heart pounding and sweat running down his face. Gradually the struggles lessened. A final spasm shook the dying body and the struggles cased altogether.

He held on a few more minutes to make completely sure, then proceeded to unstring the piano wire.

The piano wire had dug deep into the neck, making it look like a thin cord now and pieces of flesh were clinging to the wire. The eyes were bulging, almost popping out of the corpse's head in a terrified look and last minute realization of what was happening. The tongue which had swollen to a painful proportion stuck out of the mouth like an accusing finger.

Ify and Pat were still battling it out but fear and desperation gave Pat superior strength. Clouting Ify on the head with a candle that broke into pieces on contact, she was about to make a dash for the door when the sound of Puna's feet coming after her made her pause.

The sight of her dead finance made her head swim and she screamed involuntarily. Bile rose to her throat. Puna was upon her in a flash, gripping her by the throat before she could react again. Her beauty and delicate build struck him as extraordinary. He found himself swallowing hand. He hadn't noticed before how beautiful she was because of the heat that had been generated since their arrival.

What a waste of beauty! He mused. Suddenly his whole body and soul revolted against this cold-blooded murder he was about to commit. His hands began to slip away, slowly from her throat. Then she fainted in his arms.

C

Squatting by the side of the imposing Iroko tree that stood at the approach to the Bendel State Bank, Jimoh licked his lips in satisfaction as the last of the guards rubbed his eyes sleepily and crumpled to the ground in a heap. He nodded smugly at **Brian Obi** who was squatting beside him. Obi nodded back.

The two of them had been there for the past half hour, watching the guards fall asleep at their posts. One of the guards was slumped over his gun. Another who had fallen asleep with his hand in his crotch had almost made the eunuch burst into laughter.

They waited for another two minutes to make sure none of the guards was stirring. Then they got up and began walking boldly and casually along the drive to the bank. Once out of the range of view of anyone standing on the road, Jimoh drew out a blunt nosed .38 Police Positive and slid back the safety catch. Then putting his hands to his lips, he blew three low-pitched whistles, at the same time checking his watch. 10.21 p.m. The timing was perfect.

From some dry sewage disposal pipes emerged Ify, Puna and Young. They had all holed up there at the eunuch's request to come out into the open only on hearing his three low-pitched whistles. They sauntered over to where the eunuch and Obi were waiting. Watching them closely, Jimoh regretted having allowed Young go hard on a bottle of whisky. When the youngster had come back from knocking off that cop-woman, his nerves had been shot to pieces. Jimoh had allowed him a go at a bottle of whisky to calm his nerves, but looking at the youngster now, he doubted the wisdom of that action. The glassy eyes that were out of focus, the slightly open mouth . . . . the guy could start something any minute which would botch the whole operation.

"You've been drinking too much, Bill. Better watch yourself. We've come too far for this operation to be messed up. If anyone tries to make a mess of this job or stop me, I'll spread his guts on the ground." He stopped to glance at Puna. "You scout around Joe. If you happen to see any guard not asleep by chance, clout him over the head or finish him there and then. The job has been smooth so far but we're taking no chances. The stakes are too high for chances." As Joe sauntered off to where a cluster of sleeping bodies lay, "Your show now Obi." the eunuch said, a strange glint in his eyes. Whenever he participated in a job this glint was remniscent of him. "From now till we come out of the bank, you're running the show."

Obi nodded. He was wearing a green woollen sweater, light-brown slacks, heavy shoes and dark gloves over his hands. He was sweating slightly as he led the approach to the bank. The beads of perspiration on his forehead wasn't a result of the sweater. He was feeling a little scared. It had been a lot easier hatching the plans in a cosy apartment and listening to the symphony of jazz music. He knew he could get up to four hundred thousand if this job was handled right. There was so much money in this bank. The actual task of robbing the bank was something different from what he'd been dreaming of all those nights. Suppose one of those guards suddenly pops up and starts a deadly gun-play.

He paused a moment near the outer of the bank doors, listening to the acceleration of his heartbeats. It irritated him and made him feel like a lousy coward. He had always regarded himself as someone very brave. The knowledge of his present internal fears didn't augur well for such self-regard.

His gloved-hands shook as he brought out the keys. Glancing at his partners, he noted the strained, anxious faces and the fidgety, nervous movements. The eunuch was the most composed of the lot. Obi forced a smile as he inserted a key in the brass-lock of the oak door. He fiddled for some moments, growing more nervous when the door didn't open. He removed the key and one examination made him curse vilely; his nerves must be very jittery for him to be using the key upside down. He reversed the key quickly and inserted it correctly turned and the resulting click made him grunt with satisfaction. He turned the knob.

"Freeze!"

His heart bounced and then began to race madly. Slowly, his hands slipped from the brass knob. He turned round.

One of the guards stood spread-legged in front of a bunch of flowers growing at the bank entrance, his eyes sleepy but mean. He had an Enfield P 17 Rifle levelled at them, and the gaping snout looked big and ugly. He had taken only a little of the 'stuff' they have been served tonight. He had merely fallen to the ground, a bit groggy, when he heard the shuffling footsteps and the turning of the key.

"Put your hands where I can see them." He ordered in a deadly voice. "A guy who tries to rob this bank is a goner before he knows it. Smart of you, isn't it? You guys cleverly doped us. But this is the last job you'll ever pull. And don't think you can play smart with me. Make a false move and I'll blast a hole, big enough to bury a whale, in your guts. Hey big one, drop your gun." The eunuch whose fingers had been frozen on his .38 positive dropped the gun reluctantly, his lips moving unintelligibly.

The guard grinned at him sheepishly.

"Simmer down mister or you'll make my trigger finger nervous. The guy with the key . . . . . . uh!" That was as far as he got before Puna who had been creeping up behind him hit him hard with the butt of his Thompson sub-machine gun and the guy hit the ground with a sickening thud.

Obi let out a deep breath. Flashing on the torch, he opened the outer door and stepped in to the area partitioned by the two doors. The others followed quickly behind except Puna. Working quickly and more calmly now he opened the inner door and entered into the familiar hall of old. He glanced warily around, noting the old counters he used to lean on and boss over the clerks. Jimoh and the others came closely behind. They passed an intersecting door and came abruptly on the stairs leading down to the door of the vault.

There was no other source of light here apart from the torch. Stabbing the ray of light before them they proceeded to descend the stairs. At the foot of the stairs, he paused to wipe salty sweat from the corner of his mouth, then jabbed in the vault key. A wave of exhilaration hit him as he twisted the key and swung open the vault door. Still guiding himself with the torch he entered, then held the door for the others to pass. When the last of them was inside, he released the door and it closed softly behind them.

The vault was a little stuffy as the ventilator had been switched off for the day.

Flashing the light around, he spotted the crates in a corner. There were a lot of them but he didn't want to bother with those he knew would contain only cheques. He sidled over to the nearest crate and opened it. The sight of all the rolls of crisp naira bills with bands over them made his mouth water. He lifted one of the rolls and sifted it through his fingers, feeling the power of those bills. It gave him an immense thrill. It had been so long since Obi saw so much bills last.

Behind him Ify caught her breath sharply. She made a move for some rolls, her eyes shining with greed. Jimoh caught her hand an and twisted it.

"Better pocket your greed for the time being. This is no place for picking rolls."

He released her, frowning as his eyes focused on some locked crates.

"What's this mean?" He queried, fingering one of the crates.

"The new arrivals. Not yet opened." Obi replied, lifting one of the crates. It weighed as he'd expected. "We're taking only seven crates. Should be enough for all." He looked at Jimoh who nodded in assent.

Holding the torch, Obi watched as each of them lifted one crate and followed him back to the steely vault door. He pushed open the door and held it while the three filed past with their burden. Ify was having difficulty in climbing the stairs with hers. He grinned nervously. He wasn't going to help her. She had to earn her share of the steal. At every door he held it open for them while they moved past. Once past the oak door they put down the crates.

"The second trip." Obi announced immediately. He wasn't wasting time. Though the job was going on smoothly as planned, he knew that anything could happen at any moment. He didn't want to be around when it happened.

The same process was repeated during the second trip — Obi holding back the doors for them . . . .

"Two of you watch over these crates." Jimoh ordered Ify and Young. "I'm going with Obi to collect one more crate."

The two went down into the vault again and Jimoh collected one more crate — this one a little bigger than the others in size. Once outside the vault, Obi locked the door and pocketed the key. With the torch still guiding them, they climbed the stairs, past the intersecting door and the bank counters, then the glass door. Again Obi locked this up. Finally the oak door.

Meanwhile Furo Kpondo who had been observing them from a safe distance, quickly backed the ambulance out of the tangle of bushes where it had lain for twenty minutes and sped into the drive. Putting the gear in reverse again, he sent the car crawling backwards until the rear was a few inches from the crates. Then he killed the engine and got out. He'd had to go to the hospital and steal the ambulance after putting its driver to sleep. He opened the back door and they began loading on the crates. Jimoh threw the last crate he'd just brought on board, dragged out the uniforms of the ambulance attendants.

"Start changing into the uniforms quickly. We're running out of time." There was excitement in his voice — excitement arising from the knowledge that he was a few minutes from completing one of the greatest robberies in Nigerian history.

Ify picked up one of the uniforms and started moving to a corner.

"Remove your clothes there, you whore!" Jimoh snapped at her, feeling a choking rage in his chest as he threw off his clothes. "This is no time for modesty. When you've got your share you can jump into a river to remove your clothes."

Reluctantly Ify began zipping down her dress. As they finished dressing, they were joined by Puna who began changing his hurriedly.

Walking to the front of the ambulance mini-bus, Kpondo suddenly stiffened as he caught a slight movement from the corner of his eye. His heart bounced as he made a dive for the ground, shouting simultaneously.

"Get down!"

Even his dive failed to save him as automatic weapons fire started shattering, spraying tracer lead in a wide arc. Two large steel-jacketed slugs tore into his bowels and spewed out his entrails. He fell in one knee, one hand trying to gather his spewing intestines and the other clawing for the gun in his uniform. His face was contorted with pain as he brought out the gun. His dental bridge-work disappeared in a spasm of blood as another whistling slug homed in on his mouth. The gun slipped slowly from his fingers and the gurgling sound he made was lost as his head hit the tar.

The guard who had just opened fire happened to be awake by chance. He, like the former guard, hadn't taken much of the evening's supper so the dope's effect on him had been minimal. He had come awake suddenly to find a strange man hovering over them and being too afraid to move, he'd lain there pretending to be still asleep. The drug hadn't allowed him to reason properly. But even in that state he'd known something was wrong. Listening as the strange man moved away suddenly, he'd got up, glanced around to find his partners sleeping. That was when he picked up his gun, came into view and seeing these guys, even his fuddled mind knew were robbers, opened fire on them.

Meanwhile the rattle of automatic fire had sent the rest of the gang diving for cover. Even as he landed on the ground, Jimoh's .38 Positive was in his hand. Turning, flame leapt from his gun followed by a deafening bang. The slug shattered the guard's knee cap and sent him howling on the ground in pain. From inside a gutter, Puna's gun chattered on a rhythm of its own, flame licking spasmodically from it. Young and Obi had also drawn their guns and were firing at where the guard lay.

Despite his shattered knee-cap and the four guns directed at him, the brave guard kept his automatic fire going. His teeth gritted in pain and his blood flowing to the ground, he knew he would never be able to walk again. Doctors would probably amputate his leg. He didn't quite cherish walking with crutches. Life like that was intolerable to him. He rather preferred to die fighting. Maybe if he lost his life fighting these robbers, the directors of the bank would put all his children on automatic scholarship. They would be able to get the best education available ..... he hadn't been able to send any of his children to secondary school due to financial difficulties.

Cursing at the time that was being wasted, Jimoh crept out from the wall of the bank where he'd been hiding and began to crawl forward. The rage inside his chest was near to explosion. Of all the luck in the world! When the whole job was just about finished, this louse of a guard was to wake up. Above him slugs were whistling past. A slug hit the tar a little ahead of him and ricocheted past his ear. He paused to wipe sweat from his eye lashes, then changed direction at a tangent. This brought him to a flower bed in front of the bank. Using the bed as protection, he ran in a crouch to the other end of the bed from where he had an uninterrupted view of the wounded guard, who lay defiantly in pain at one end of the building. The guard stiffened instinctively and tried to swing his gun hurriedly but he had left it a moment too late.

Jimoh's first shot tore off the man's genitals making him double over in excruciating pain. Running forward lightly, his second slug, fired at point blank range, penetrated the man's brain killing him instantly. Not stopping to make sure the guard was dead, he sprinted for where Kpondo lay, shouting at the same instant.

"You guys get into the ambulance quickly! There is no time to waste! Bill, take over the wheel!" He turned Kpondo over on his back and didn't bother to feel the pulse. Lifting the dead body, he carried it to the back of the ambulance and threw it inside.

The others were already bundled inside. Jumping inside, he closed the door.

"Full speed, Bill! Full speed!"

The engine came into life and the ambulance mini-bus lurched forward, then spun on the tar with a screeching of tires. Young brought it back on course and held it steady until they came to where the drive merged with the major road. As the vehicle spun into the major road, there was the scream of a siren behind and next moment mayhem was let loose.

The Police patrol car came to a hair-raising stop and even before it stopped, Policemen were spilling out of it and coming at them, their guns hammering. A rifle barked. A Tommy-gun chattered and a pistol banged. Red-hot slugs splattered the get-away vehicle, drawing gaping holes in the thin plates. A slug twanged past Jimoh's face and then he felt a searing pain shoot up his left shoulder. He groaned in pain and involuntarily, obscenities flowed from his mouth. Bringing up his .38 Positive he manoeuvred his head out of the window and sighted along its barrel. The gun barked in his hand and he saw a cop thrown backwards into the dust.

A chain of slugs tore into the vehicle's rear off-side tire bursting it in one huge rush of air and making the ambulance veer wildly in the direction of the bush. Young fought desperately with the steering, struggling to bring the vehicle back into control. Finally he managed to steady the vehicle on their course but the speed had reduced considerably.

"Give her more fire! Fire!" Jimoh raved, saliva dribbling from the corners of his mouth.

"I can't get it to respond more than this," Young shouted above the din of shooting.

"You're bleeding badly, Gilt." Ify commented, looking at him worriedly.

"Don't worry about me I can look after myself." He glanced briefly at the blood that was seeping from the wound and soaking his clothes, then his hawkish eyes returned to the road. The cops, still shooting on the run, were gaining fast after their vehicle which was crawling at less than 10 m.p.h. A gasp of pain made him whip around.

A lump of shrapnel had pried open Obi's chest and blood was flowing freely. The former Bank Manager dipped a finger in the blood and shook his head sadly. Ify rushed over to a medical kit in a corner and picked it up. He waved her away.

"No need, sister. When a man takes a lump of shrapnel in his heart, his days are numbered." He stooped to wipe his bloody fingers on the leg of his trouser, then picked up his fallen .32 automatic from the floor of the ambulance. He regarded Jimoh with a forced smile. "I'm finished, Gilt. I know it, wouldn't last much longer. It was I who lured you into deciding to pull this job so I guess I've got to try pulling you out of this mess. Tell Young to slow down some more so that I can jump off. I'll try to keep these lousy cops occupied. Maybe you guys can still escape."

"No!" Jimoh said sharply. "We're all in this together. I won't have you making yourself a sacrifical lamb. You'll still survive. We'll get a doctor later. The wound is nothing to lose hope about . . . . . just a slight graze."

Obi's blood was now flowing in the ambulance. His voice was sad as he spoke with finality.

"Good luck to you, Gilt. If you guys escape, my effort wouldn't have been in vain. If not . . . . tough luck."

"Brian!" Jimoh shouted, shoving the goggle-eyed Ify out of the way and lounging to grab him. But he slipped on the pool of blood and fell. When he managed to get up, it was already too late.

Opening the side door, Obi jumped with all his remaining strength, breaking his fall on the sidewalk with a twist of his shoulders but nevertheless feeling a jarring pain on his shoulder blade. He was rolling as he hit the sidewalk, getting only a glimpse at the vehicle that was battling on. A bullet buzzed past him. A Tommy-gun spat death at him but the ricocheting slugs whistled harmlessly past. The pain in his belly was unbearable now. Bringing up his .32 automatic, he grinned as the gun belched flame and thundered. One of the cops took the slug on the run and pitched forward onto the road, blood leaking from his mouth. Not waiting to see the cop fall, Obi's gun roared again and again. The second bullet took another cop in midstride and he fell to the tar breaking his jaw. There was the blast of a shrill whistle and immediately the remaining cops stopped running and turned their fire power on him.

Obi was rolling into the gutter when a slug twisted off one of his toes. Falling into the gutter he winced in pain. The gutter was a little deep and offered him temporary shelter from the barrage of slugs searching for him. Cannons boomed. Machine guns chattered. Lugers barked. Bringing up his head a little, he grinned. The ambulance was escaping as he wanted. A bullet ploughed through his hair. He lay back, hearing the patter of slugs on the pavement. He knew the time wouldn't be long before the policemen rushed to the gutter. Once they got over their first reaction of fear when he'd knocked down two of their fold, they would surely come. Raising his hand a little, he fired a shot to keep them at bay. The he began to crawl in the gutter, his face in the grime. The dirt stank in his nose and entered his mouth. When he'd crawled to an intersection point with a bigger gutter he glanced back.

The cops were all over the spot where he'd lain before. Congratulating himself for his smart move, he threw himself into the bigger gutter. He lay there, his heart beating sluggishly and trying to get back his breath. There was a concrete slab covering the gutter for about three yards. He could hear the sound of running feet coming nearer. He brought up his head and fired another shot, forcing the cops to dive for cover. Even as he withdrew his head, a bullet ploughed a furrow along his cheek.

Cursing vehemently the former banker crawled under the cement slab. His strength was ebbing fast. There were heavy footsteps on the slab now.

A voice shouted into the gutter. "We know you're there, mister. You'd better crawl out now with your hands on your head or we'll riddle your hole with lead."

Obi turned on his side and raising his clothes, inspected the wound in his chest. It looked ugly and big with grime on it. The sight of it made his head swim. What was he waiting for? Was he waiting for them to capture him and make him live again? So that they could get useful statements from him Even if he survived, he would still face a firing squad. Any armed robber in this country was living on borrowed time. Once nabbed no way out, brother.

Money! Money! Naira bills! What money can do to a man! Millions of naira had been so near and yet so far away. He didn't think Jimoh and his gang would make it. Maybe they would get away for a day or two. But they wouldn't get far. The law would apprehend them. The scheme he'd so intricately concocted had blown up in his face. And once the law latches unto you, you're a goner.

He saw a slight movement from the corner of his eye – two policemen jumping into the gutter simultaneously and spraying his 'hole' with slugs. He tried to get his gun handy quickly. A slug slammed into his skull. Two more slammed into his chest. Dazed, he glanced at the blotches on his clothes, then putting the gun into his mouth, he blew his brains out.

Meanwhile as the ambulance bus sped on, Jimoh could hear the stacatto bursts of gunfire from a safe distance. He knew Obi wouldn't make it. The shrapnel in his chest had been fatal. The realization of that fact had driven Obi to make that courageous sacrifice. And how the guy had succeeded!

Observing their rear he allowed a grim, sad smile to play at the corners of his mouth. The cops were nowhere in sight. The thrill of having pulled off one of the greatest robberies ever had soured a little. Maybe it was the knowledge that someone had sacrificed himself to make sure he got away with the take. It wasn't usual for him to feel the loss of a human life. Since he lost his potency, such common things never made him lose a wink of sleep. In fact, he'd been participating in destroying lives.

"There's a long line of cars ahead." Young's slightly musical voice broke into Jimoh's thoughts. "What do I do, Gilt?"

Jimoh screwed up his face in concentration. His reply was slow in coming. "Put on the sirene. We'll pretend it's an emergency and pass all these cars. When we reach the road-block, if they don't allow us immediate passage, try to bluff our way out. You're a smooth talker so that's right up your alley. Try to rattle them with big talk but if you see they're not going to give up, then jam the accelerator to the floor; we'll shoot our way out."

Young nodded, then put the sirens at full blast. With the light blinking, he sent the Volks mini-bus screaming past the long line of cars. There weren't any cars coming from the opposite direction yet so he had easy passage. As he neared the road-block, he slowed down gradually, with the sirens still blaring shrilly. His heart was thumping as a uniformed armed policeman sidled over to the ambulance window and glanced in at him.

"What's happening here, mister?" Young demanded heavily. "Why aren't vehicles moving? A hold up or something?"

The policeman shrugged. "Curfew breakers in the main. But there's been some shooting going on that way — probably near the bank. Could be some nut has dreamt and is trying to rob the bank. Me, I wouldn't worry myself if some crazy fellow decides to give the bank a try. Too much bread in that bank. Time someone gave those jerks working in the bank something to worry about." He laughed gaily then looked at Young more seriously. "Aren't you coming from that direction?"

"Sure, I'm just coming from that side. Heard some shooting behind me and a lot of smoke going up. Didn't have the time to wait and see what was wrong . . . . I'm carrying an emergency case here."

"Oh. Serious eh?"

"Yeah. The patient's in a coma."

"In that case we'd better give the vehicle a quick going over. We're searching all cars coming from that direction. The law breakers could be in one of these vehicles. My boss's orders. Nothing much but mere routine."

Young felt his palm go moist on the steering wheel. His heart was bumping at a fast rate and he had to wet his lips which had suddenly gone dry. Making an effort to hide the slight tremor in his voice, he spoke:

"This is an emergency, mister. Tell those guys to lower the chain. I'd better be moving. My patient needs immediate medical attention."

The cop's eyes hardened. "I've got my orders and I'm carrying them out. My job. If you don't like it, then protest to my boss." He began walking towards the back of the vehicle.

"Hey!" Young's shout was now final and desperate.

The cop came back.

"You know something? My patient is an influential one. If he dies before I get to the hospital, then you'll be in big trouble. The trouble could be big enough that your boss wouldn't be able to handle it. Then he could throw you to the wolves and deny that he ever gave you an order to delay an ambulance."

The cop was rattled. An instant reaction came over his face and he looked like one who had just eaten a spider.

"Who said I was trying to delay an ambulance?" His tone had softened. "All I wanted was to peep inside. Didn't mean to delay you. Go right along." He waved at the man holding the chain and the guy lowered it.

Young put the vehicle in gear. He was jubilant. "I know you didn't mean to delay me; but better watch it. Next time you try to get wise I could have you booted out of the Force. You'll be crawling on the ground in this city begging for food."

The top, standing on his tip toes, glanced into the Volks as it sped past, but there was nothing unusual to alert his suspicions. Ify and Puna had cleverly brought the boxes together, placed the stretcher on it and Jimoh was laid on the stretcher. Kpondo's body was placed in a sitting position on one of the seats and all the guns had been hidden under the seats.

Once past the road-block, Young glanced back and grinned. One and half million Naira! The thought of this money at the back made him water his pants involuntarily.

VI

A

Omo Baba knocked twice on the door leading to his chief's office, then swaggered in. The deep Persian rug on the tiled floor muffled his steps. Reaching his chief's table, he stuck out a foot and drew a chair towards him. Sitting down heavily, he regarded his chief who was sitting opposite him and hadn't looked up since he entered.

Ogunbor's bulk filled a straight leather-backed chair and he sat, engrossed in the contents of a report. Naked fatigue was etched on his face — there were rings under his eyes and his face looked closely drawn. As he pored over the pages of the report, Baba could notice a nervous tic on his left cheek. Finally he looked up from the report and regarded his erstwhile detective.

"Heard you wanted me, sir."

Ogunbor nodded. He proceeded to pick up a pipe from one corner of his desk which was littered with papers. He lit the pipe, then stuck it in a corner of his mouth.

"Come up with anything yet?" He asked slowly as he blew out smoke.

Baba shrugged. "Little. Could be outright trash? we'll soon see. The investigation is just starting. I'm hoping there would be further developments. Without that we wouldn't move an inch."

Ogunbor leaned back in his chair, then raised his naked feet onto the desk. He looked shrewd as he stared at Baba.

"From what you have so far, what do you make of the case?

Think we'll be able to catch the robbers?"

Baba let his mind wander back to the events of the previous night. After a very tiring day trying to develop a lead to the high way robbers who'd waylaid Aina, robbed and murdered him, he'd come back to the office to type his report. Sitting on the chair his mind had invariably flirted to his encounter with the fortune-teller, he'd kept wondering whether the old man's warning was to be taken seriously. He'd fallen asleep in the process and had suddenly awakened to the sound of heavy shooting. Looking up drowsily, he'd found corporal Jim Okuns standing over him.

"What are you waiting for?" Okuns had asked. "There's shooting going on near the bank. Seems some lunatics have decided to rob the bank. Some of the boys have rushed to investigate."

Baba sprang out of the chair like a mamba, his sleep and fatigue forgotten. On the way down the stairs, he'd paused to make sure the gun was in its leather holster. He drove furiously towards the bank and stopped some metres from where the skirmish was taking place. Running in a crouch, a bullet had zipped past his ear. He had missed most of the action for when he finally got there, one robber had blown his brains out and events had been moving speedily since then. It had taken Baba a few minutes to get a run down of the battle. He had quickly dispatched two of the cops to the road-block to inform the guy in charge there to stop any ambulance from passing through. To his dismay he'd learnt later on that the men had passed just a few minutes before the order came. A pursuit was organised but came up with nothing.

Going back to the bank, the sleeping guards had told him one thing — that this was a cleverly organised robbery. He'd simply stopped all proceedings there to wait for Ogunbor. They'd later found some keys on the robber who'd committed suicide and from there, it was almost apparent the bank had been robbed. The Police chief had then ordered that nothing more should be touched at the bank until he gave the order. He'd left some new guards at the bank and the 'sleeping ones' carted off to the Force Headquarters.

Finally Baba cleared his throat and spoke.

"What we have at this juncture points to the fact that the mob managed to get across to the guards somehow and doped them. This gave them unhampered access to the bank." The intercom buzzed just then and Ogunbor picked up the telephone.

"The Bank Manager is here, sir." Okuns spoke into the telephone. "Do I send him in?"

"Sure, send him in straight away." He turned to Baba and offered him a slight smile. "The Bank Manager is here. I think we'll start making substantial headways soon."

A minute later, the door opened and a man entered the room. He was middle-aged with a big head for figures that depicts a lot of financial connections. In this business you ran often into rich guys who would try to bulldoze you into seeing things from their own perspective. His skin was a little lighter than ebony-black and he walked erect and with dignity. He had on a nicely cut suit and a tie.

Baba got up from the chair, mumbled a greeting and offered him the chair. A courteous thanks and then the Manager shook hands across the table with Ogunbor.

"Glad to see you, Mr. Okosun," Ogunbor was saying. "Sit down. Sit down."

Okosun sat down and adjusted his tie. He regarded the Police Chief with scorn.

"You've been to the bank eh?" Ogunbor asked.

The Bank Manager nodded.

"Just coming from there now. Your secretary gave me the keys."

Baba, pen and note book in hand, was already scribbling down. "Anything missing?"

"You asking if something is missing?" The Manager demanded, ready to explode any minute. He'd been under some mental stress from the time he learnt of the doping of the guards from Corporal Okuns. "You ever seen a toad jumping about in the day time for nothing? Do you imagine they couldn't have robbed the bank, when the guards were sleeping? Sure! They made off with seven crates of raw cash. That's approximately two million naira."

Ogunbor sucked in his breath. Two million naira! The hoodlums in this city were becoming too daring for his liking.

"You get it now? Two million naira! That could ruin the bank!"

"Easy. Easy. Take it easy." The Police Chief advised. "We're merely trying to get the records straight. If you co-operate there's still some hope we would nab the robbers."

Okosun simmered down a bit. "So what do you want to know?"

Ogunbor thought for some time. "Let's go over the bank's security arrangements starting from the time you hand the keys over to us. I'd like to refresh my memory."

"At five p.m.," Okosun began, "a set of twenty-four guards arrive to take over the human side of the security system. Meanwhile the four guards who keep watch during the day and myself bring the keys over to this place and hand them over. The twenty-four guards keep watch till eight p.m. At eight, twelve of the guards would go to the canteen and have a light supper while the remaining twelve keep watch. Ten minutes later the former twelve come back to resume watch while the latter go for their own supper. The whole thing takes ten minutes. So at 8.20 p.m. the whole twenty-four are keeping watch again until when I arrive in the morning which is at 8. a.m." He paused to stare at the police chief. "I'm positive no one could have broken into that bank without putting those guards out of action."

"How about the bank itself? I mean the inanimate side of the security system."

"One thing, to get to the money in the vault one has to pass not less than three security locked doors, including the vault door. The only silent way into that vault is the bank keys. Anyone who tries to use any instruments like all these picks will set off a huge alarm which could be heard here at Police Headquarters. The guys who robbed that bank didn't break in. They had the keys to those doors."

Which makes you one of the suspects, Ogunbor reflected inwardly. Watching Okosun grimly, he jerked out a drawer and threw a set of keys on the table.

"Check those keys." He told him.

Okosun picked up the keys. His eyes began going over them and suddenly he started back.

"Where, where did you get these keys?" He asked in a visibly shaken voice. "These are exact duplicates of the bank keys I carry. The person who had these keys cast must have had access to the original keys." His eyes were suddenly accusing. "You didn't have anything to do with the casting, I hope?"

Ogunbor relaxed. This man couldn't have had anything to do with the robbery unless he was a damn good actor.

"Shove it." He said. "Those keys were found in the pocket of one of the robbers. He was dead when we found him. Committed suicide in the shoot-out. He's now in the mortuary. We're seeking an identification, which should be difficult considering that some parts of his head was blown away. The pathologist is working on his face so that we can take a presentable picture of it. We intend to circulate pictures of him later."

The telephone rang. Ogunbor picked it up.

"The body of a woman has just been found." Corporal Okuns said. "Found clubbed to death in an alley. Constable Braimoh just reported. Told him to wait while I informed you."

"Okay, get the doctor and the laboratory attendants on the job. Sergeant Jumbo should handle this. I'm busy now."

As he replaced the receiver, Okosun got up. "I'm going back to the bank now. If you want me later I'll be available."

Ogunbor escorted him to the door, said goodbye and closed the door after him. He walked back slowly to his desk. "This case is going to be a complicated one, Omo." The Police Chief said. "The doctor has checked some of those sleeping guards. He sent samples of their blood to the laboratory some time ago. Said the results should be ready sometime this afternoon. While waiting for the results and further developments, let's do some analysis. What do you make of the Bank Manager?"

Baba shrugged. "He looks clean but I could be wrong. One never can tell where money is concerned."

The Chief nodded. "How about the whole operation?"

"Smells. From what the Bank Manager said it is evident no one could have robbed that bank without inside help. I'm betting the guys who robbed it had a fore-knowledge of the security network there. First, they managed to dope those guards. It's my guess that the guard who was killed might have seen the robbers or intercepted them especially as he died from gun shot wounds. Probably if it hadn't been for him those robbers could have got off easily. Secondly, these keys are the exact replicas of the ones to that bank and if again we're to go by what the Manager said, who ever had those keys cast, had access to the original ones. Which points again to an inside accomplice. It's my opinion that this job was cleverly organised. They even used an ambulance as their get-away vehicle. Fooled those jerks at that road-block."

"That reminds me, did you get anything out of that creep who allowed those robbers to pass without searching them?"

"Little. The guy said he had been emphatic about searching the ambulance but the driver told him he was in a hurry, that he was carrying an influential patient who was in a coma. Said the driver went further to threaten him that if the patient died, he was going to get kicked out of the force. At that stage he gave way. He didn't see much of the driver except that he was wearing the uniform of an ambulance attendant. However when I pressed him to think more, he remembered the guy had a musical voice. He concluded by saying he took a peep at the ambulance as it went past and noticed a form laid out on a stretcher inside. Said it was that which wholly convinced him."

"We're up against a clever criminal." The Police Chief commented acidly.

Baba felt a stab of jealousy. He always experienced this stab whenever his Chief complimented another man especially when it was for a criminal giving them some headache.

"The criminal may not be as clever as we make out," he said carefully, smothering the sharp edge that was creeping into his voice. "A guy with as much brains as a toad could have robbed that bank if he gave it enough thought."

Ogunbor covered up a smile by yawning. This streak of jealousy in Baba had always amused him. He almost felt like prodding Baba further but the problem at hand made him defer it. Just then the telephone rang again.

It was the director of Benin General Hospital, phoning to tell him that one of their ambulance vehicles — a Volkswagen Mini-bus was missing.

Ogunbor stiffened, then expectation bells began jangling inside his head. "When was it discovered missing?" Inside his head he was thinking that this could be an unexpected break.

"Early this morning. The driver of the ambulance reported it. said he was clouted on the head around nine or thereabouts last night. When he woke up, he was lying in a little bush, with his head aching and the ambulance gone."

"Did he say he saw the man who hit him on the head?"

"Said he couldn't quite remember. All he could remember was seeing a dark blur and next moment he was out. Think you'd be able to find the ambulance?"

"Maybe. I'm not promising anything but we just could find it."

"You've got to do better than that. There's only one ambulance van left in the hospital now. This missing one's got to be found. We're facing financial hardships at the moment, so purchasing another vehicle is out of the question."

"I've told you before, I'm not promising anything but we just could find it. This is a big city so better not hope much. Even if we find it, the damn thing may not be of much use to you any longer."

"What do you mean?" The Director's voice coming from the other end of the line was rattled.

"If I have anything for you later I'll inform you. What's the number of the ambulance?"

There was a pause down the line then, "BB 1345X."

"Thanks." He wrote down the number. "We'll work on that. Anything else?"

"Nothing. Aw, wait a minute. I hope you won't mind my being inquisitive?"

"Go ahead. I'll help you if I can." The Police Chief replied.

"I heard there was a shoot-out at the Bendel State Bank last night. Some guys tried to rob the bank?"

Ogunbor felt his chest contract into a fight knot. All these rich slobs who don't do anything but gossip and embezzle funds. He barely managed to choke back his rage.

"Yeah." He replied. "The rogues actually succeeded in robbing the bank." Pausing a little to allow the gist sink in, he said. "This amublance driver who was hit over the head, I'll like to have him interrogated over last night's event. One of my men will be coming over later in the day. I'll be contacting you again soon. So long."

He didn't wait to find out if the Director was finished but put down the phone immediately. The rich guys in this city always had their ears open for news and gossip. Though amusing, this at times irritated him. What more with the mood he was in this morning, it had produced outright rage.

He glanced up to meet the inquiring look of Baba. Smiling, he tossed the sheet of paper where he'd written the ambulance number to him.

"I think we're slipping up, you know." The Chief said. "To think that all this while it didn't occur to any of us to suggest contacting all the hospitals to get the ambulance number."

Baba shrugged in his usual way. "Such things happen. When the heat is on, one tends to forget things."

"Heat or no heat it just won't do if we keep forgetting things." He stared thoughtfully at Baba for some seconds, then said: "I think we'll postpone our analysis for the time being. You'd better be going to the bank now. Quiz them proper. Maybe you'll be able to establish a lead to that inside help. I've a hunch that this inside help is going to be the key to this robbery. Once we're got him, then the robbers are half-cooked."

Baba stood up and began walking towards the door. As he reached the door the intercom on Ogunbor's desk began to buzz. He paused, his hand on the knob as his Chief picked up the phone.

"Jim Okuns, sir." The excited voice of the corporal said over the phone. "Sergeant Jumbo just reported that he's identified the woman who was found clubbed to death in an alley." He paused. "She's Bisi Eyo — the policewoman."

"A policewoman!" Ogunbor exclaimed. "Is Jumbo positive she's a policewoman?"

"Yeah. He was quite sure of it."

"What did you say her name was?" He queried for he hadn't heard her name the first time.

"Bisi Eyo." Okuns said, then added elaborately. "The woman who takes supper every evening to the guards at the Bendel State Bank."

The Police Chief felt a jolt under the heart, like he'd been punched there. He gripped the telephone for some moments and when he finally regained his voice, said. "Tell Jumbo to halt all proceedings. Baba is taking over. This could have something to do with the bank robbery."

He slammed down the phone, a strange light in his eyes. Having been watching him closely, Baba's instinct told him that something big was in the air. Without waiting, he closed the door and began walking back to the desk.

"Something up, Chief?"

His eyes glittered as he stared at Baba. "Sergeant Jumbo just reported he had identified a woman who was knocked off in an alley. She's a policewoman, Bisi Eyo."

Watching Baba closely, he saw understanding flood into his eyes. "The nickel's dropped? Yes, I knew you'd remember her. It possibly couldn't be mere coincidence between her death and the robbing of the Bendel State Bank. It's my guess that the robbers got her one way or the other to dope the guard's supper. Then they knocked her off knowing that once the robbery was discovered and the drugging came into light, we were likely to latch unto her in no time. A smart move on their part. The mood I'm in now, a wall would crack under my pressure."

Baba could see the link all right. Even a mug wouldn't fail to see it. Twenty-four guards watching over a bank were drugged — the whole lot of them and the bank robbed. The most likely way all of them could have gotten drugged at the same time was through the supper they ate in two groups every evening. And the woman who administered the supper was found in the morning after the robbery — clubbed to death in an alley.

"That's what I said before, even a guy with a toad's brain could have robbed that bank once he set out to do it and gave it enough thought. Just like taking sweets from a kid." He paused and regarded his Chief. "I suppose you're sending me out to the alley?"

Ogunbor nodded. "You're handling the case. Try to do as much groundwork as possible and find out all you can about her past activities — especially last night. If you have to squeeze the neighbours hard to get this information, do it. We can't afford to miss this track. Could lead to greener pastures. After that you go to the bank and quiz them too." His eyes twinkled as he stared at Baba. "You'd better dig up something we could use. I've a meeting with the Police Commissioner at eleven. He'd be screaming his head off for blood but I'll try and stall him for some time. I can't stall him forever so we'll be needing what you can dig up. A huge reward awaits you if you can find out something that would lead us to those robbers. I'll be seeing you around two."

"A reward!" Baba exclaimed, his eyes suddenly turning shrewd. "Who's giving the reward? The bank?"

"I'll see the Bank Manager about that. The bank will have to dig up some amount. Something like ten thousand."

Ten thousand! Baba thought. That was more than his yearly salary. With that kind of money he could . . . ." "See that he puts up the reward, Chief." He said in a croaky voice. "I'll find those robbers if it's the last thing I do," and he galloped out of the room.

B

Gilt Jimoh finished his breakfast, laid down the cutlery carefully and wiped his mouth with the back of his hand. He couldn't remember ever having such a good breakfast. It was simply one of the most delicious meals he'd ever had. He hadn't known Ify could cook so well. It came as a pleasant surprise to him.

Pushing the plates aside he leaned back in the chair and belched gently. He watched Ify, who'd been hovering over the table gather the plates and cup. She carried them away. As she walked away, he watched her heavy behind gyrating with an inviting firmness that made his mouth water. But his sexual organs couldn't react.

He found himself hating Puna — for the mere reason that Puna should be enjoying the things he would never enjoy again. His mind went back to last night. They had successfully returned to this apartment after the robbery. He had been fatigued by the loss of blood resulting from his arm injury. Ify had treated the arm, then bandaged it while Puna and Young carried the crates of money into the house. The ambulance was now safely in the garage with Kpondo's body still inside. Though it had pained him having to lose a member of the gang — the euphoria of all the money that would now come to him had quickly smothered the pain. Each of the surviving members would get the two hundred and fifty thousand bread they'd agreed on. The rest of the money would be his. The main obstacle to that plan was going to be Puna. He knew that Puna didn't fear him as much as did the others. In fact he'd been suspecting for some time that Puna wanted to be the boss of the gang.

"I'd better watch him carefully," he told himself. The guy could be getting ideas. Before, he hadn't given much hoot to his suspicions. But with all the money around, last night he'd watched everyone carefully. The glint in Puna's eyes when they had finished packing the crates in the house had warned him. Tried as much as he did to curtail the suspicions which were soaring to uncontrollable heights, it had all been in vain. His sharp, photographic memory couldn't forget so easily that look of pure greed that glinted with a cunning savagery. In fact, with all that money around, he couldn't trust any of his gang not to get ideas. He was going to watch them.

When Ify had finished tending to him last night, he'd gone to bed. His original plan was to stay up in bed and wait to see if Puna or anybody for that matter would start something. But he'd been too fatigued from the loss of blood and had quickly fallen asleep. By the time he woke up this morning, all the others had breakfasted.

Ify came out of the kitchen drying her hands on a towel.

"Where's Joe and Bill?" He asked, standing up from the chair.

"Outside. Playing cards."

"Go and call them. We're going to count the money now. I want everyone to be present."

As she went outside, he began walking thoughtfully to the room where the crates were packed. A slight noise from one of the rooms made him start back. It had been a stifled whimper. Getting a grip on himself he approached the door cautiously. Pausing outside the door he took in a deep breath, then turned the knob and threw the door back.

And there was Pat Ola! She lay back on the bed, her hands taped to the sides and a gag covering her mouth. He stood staring at her for some seconds, his rage swelling. The bastards! He had told them to kill her and they had disobeyed his order. He swore softly and stepped forward, his hands aching to strangle her.

"Gilt!"

He stopped in midstride. Something in the voice warned him.

"What's it Joe?" He asked, without turning round.

"Leave her alone."

"I told you guys to knock her off last night. Why didn't you do it? You fallen in love with her or something?"

"Maybe." A pause then, "leave her alone."

"Don't be a dope. Who said I was going to touch her anyway?"

"I know. You didn't intend to touch her." There was a disdain in his voice that made the eunuch's eyes glitter in suppressed rage. "I've always known you had homicidal tendencies and a eunuch's vengeful complex. If you touch her she'll be the last woman you'll touch on earth."

The eunuch spun around, his lips curled back in vicious rage. "Don't talk to me like that Joe!" His voice had a cool harshness that was packed with deadly venom. "Unless you want to die a most horrible death."

Puna laughed easily and patted the .38 positive in its leather holster around his waist. He was leaning against the door.

"This is the only gun in the house at the moment. I've packed all the other guns to a safe place where you can't get at them. Don't think you can kid with me or try something funny. Maybe you'll manage to stab me once before I blast open your guts. It would be messy, wouldn't it? Better don't play smart."

"Tell me you've been drinking and I'll forget you ever said anything." Jimoh retorted tactically. Then on further thought, added. "Where's Buko's body? I was too tired last night to ask."

Puna allowed himself a rueful smile. "I know you're a smart guy. But listen to me; never play smart when the odds are stacked against you. I'm running this gang now. Buko's body is now in the ambulance; with Furo's. You and Bill will bury them later; when we've finished counting the money. Try anything smart and see where it will land you."

Jimoh stared at him disconcertingly but the ex-soldier's eyes refused to budge. His hand hovered a few inches from the leather holster. Finally the eunuch shrugged.

"Okay, let's go count the money as you've said. Doesn't matter much if you run the gang. Maybe you're tired of life."

"Try anything funny and we'll see who is tired of life."

Puna waited until Jimoh had passed, then followed him. Young and Ify were already opening the crates as the two of them came in. As the first crate opened, Ify gasped at the sight of all that money. She knelt down, staring at the money for a long time, her eyes popping and mouth hanging open. Unable to resist the urge any longer, she dipped her hands into the crate and laddled as much of the wads as she could and pressed them to her cheeks. The bills were new, cool and she closed her eyes as the power of the bills diffused into her cheeks.

Jimoh gave her a kick on the arse. "Get up you bitch! The only thing you ever think about is money."

"Leave her alone!" Puna snarled, a dangerous glint in his eyes. "The earlier you get used to the fact you're no longer the boss around here, the better."

Ify got up and looked at the eunuch sullenly but she was scared to utter the vile words that were welling up in her throat.

Two hours and fifteen minutes later they had finished counting the money. Six of the crates contained two hundred and fifty thousand each while the last crate which contained ten naira bills only housed five-hundred thousand naira. When they have finished, Ify's greedy eyes looked up with pride.

"Two million bread! That's a whale of money. If someone had told me I would turn rich overnight I wouldn't have believed him.

"You're rich now so you'd better believe him." Puna chipped in authoritatively. "With thrèe hundred thousand Naira you can afford to . . . ."

"Three hundred thousand?" Her querrulous voice had gone up a note.

"I'm being generous. Fifty thousand more than Gilt would have allowed you."

"No." She said obstinately. "We all robbed the bank together and shared the hazards equally. Furo and Obi's shares will be split equally."

He grinned at her. "Three hundred thousand for two of you. Four hundred thousand for Gilt. The rest for me."

Young glared at him, his young face contorted with indignation. "When did you start running this gang? Let's not have any trouble over the sharing. Everyone gets the same thing and we go our separate ways."

Puna's grin widened. He suddenly realized that with all this money around it was going to be difficult to control any person in this mob. He figured that he needed time for what he was planning and the only way to get that time was to stall these people for some time. This was going to require a lot of wile.

"I was merely pulling your legs. Wanted to see your reactions." He lifted his hands helplessly.

"No one is running this gang now. We're all free to do what we like. Two million split in four gives half a million each. That's what each of us is going to get. All the plans Gilt made before are being reversed. We'll split the money tomorrow whether the heat has cooled off or not." He paused a moment and regarded Young. "What do you say, Bill?"

Young shrugged. "All right by me." He stared shrewdly at Puna who returned it. "But I'd better tell you that with all this money around it would pay everyone well to leave off pulling legs."

"Ify . . . . how about you?"

Ify had noticed that since last night, Joe hadn't so much as given her a genuine smile. After Jimoh had retired to bed, he had been very preoccupied with the 'Pat' dame. He had stayed with the dame for the rest of the night. She had come in unexpectedly to catch Joe nibbling at the girl's breasts and it had taken only one look at his eyes for her to discover he was in love. When she had tried to protest, the way his eyes changed dangerously had made her scared. She had quickly taken her exit from the room. One thing was apparent to her now — that she could no longer trust Joe. Whatever he was planning, and she was positive he was playing a smart game, he didn't intend to let her in.

If there was one thing Ify had in abundance it was wile. She knew that this game of waiting and double-crossing was not for amateurs — least of all women. She had to have someone . . . . a man to lean on if she was going to get anything when the clash came. Joe didn't want her again so he was out. Gilt was strong and smart . . . . a cool pro, and probably the smartest of the lot but he had no time for her so he was out too. That left Bill. Fast with a gun and loquacious — but he still had some streaks of amateurism in him. He had a yearning for anything in skirts. She had better team up with him. If the two of them joined forces maybe they would provide a strong front.

"What's on your mind?" Joe demanded suspiciously. He had the uncomfortable feeling that Ify suspected he was planning something. "I asked your opinion. You haven't given it."

"Anything Bill says is all right by me." She had made up her mind to join forces with him! "He's a smart guy. Should know what is good for all of us." Her lashes went up and she looked at Bill coyly.

Recognising that look Bill held her eyes for a moment, then his lips curled into a smile. He know he now had a new ally and a bedmate.

Joe noticed the conspiratorial exchange of looks and his fists clenched instinctively. So some dopes were envisaging putting up a united front against him. Well let them. If they so much as presented a threat to his plans he would rub them off. But he wasn't worrying about them. It was Gilt that he worried most about. Every aspect of Gilt was formidable — even if ruthlessly or cold-bloodedly formidable. If there was one guy he would watch out for, it was Gilt. The path he'd chosen was fraught with dangers. But for all this money he would take on a lion barehanded.

"How about you Gilt?" He asked. "The decision okay by you?"

The eunuch shrugged coolly. "Why should I care? We're all getting half a million. That's a lot of money. One couldn't ask for more."

Joe knew the eunuch was lying. He stared at him for a long moment, trying to pierce through that expressionless mask to discover what was going on in that razor-sharp brain. But the eunuch's face betrayed nothing.

Joe suddenly grinned. At times he was forced to admire the eunuch's calm in the face of tribulation.

"You know something Gilt? You're a bloody good actor. I'd give you that. But this time you've left your plan too late."

"What plan?" The eunuch faked indignance.

"Aw come on Gilt, don't think you can con me. I know you're planning something. But watch out. A wrong step and I'll drill you full of holes. One can't risk taking chances with all this money around."

Jimoh had to struggle to check himself. He suddenly hated Joe more than he had ever hated any guy before. He knew the ex-soldier wasn't kidding. Joe would knock him off at the slightest excuse. The guy had the gun all along and would still play it cool for some time not to give him any excuse to kill. He would bid his time until the ripe opportunity came, then he would fling all the venom in him at the ex-soldier. He knew Joe's reputation. Once he had set his mind on something an excuse was enough to bump someone . . . .

There came the sound of heavy banging on the door leading outside.

VII

A

Fifteen minutes later the powerful squad car was winding its way along the narrow dirt-littered road. There were a lot of pot-holes on this road so Baba had to wrestle with the steering and endure the harsh bumps in order to maintain a reasonable speed.

Finally he steered the car into the grounds opposite the alley. There were many people gathered near the mouth of the alley. As he got out of the car, one of the policemen wandered over to his side.

"Where's Jumbo?" He asked the smart-looking young policeman.

"In his squad car, where those by-standers are clustered. He's been waiting for you."

Treading his way carefully among the crowd, he managed to get to the open space just before the squad car. In the open space was a form draped over with a sheet. He didn't raise the sheet immediately but allowed his eyes to scan the environs. The ambulance was parked nearest the form. The back door was open and some of the attendants sat inside, waiting. Beside the ambulance was the squad car, with Jumbo leaning on the door in deep conversation with Doctor John Moziah.

Jumbo grinned on seeing him. He seemed relieved that this wasn't going to be his cup of tea. The men shook hands.

"I don't know what is happening to this goddamn city. Seems everything's going to pieces."

Baba shrugged in his usual noncommital way.

"Let's go see the body." He said.

The trio walked over to where the sheet-covered form lay. As Jumbo raised the sheet, his face screwed up in a grimace and the crowd pressed forward curiously, craning their necks to see the body. The policemen holding them back had a tough job on their hands.

Baba's hands clenched unconsciously at the sight of the body, his eyes going sightless for a moment. When the wave of dizziness finally abated, he inspected the body more closely.

The eyes were slightly open with an expression of terror in them. Her lips were drawn back over her teeth, like she had been about to curse her killer when she died. The side of her head was battered almost to pulp. One of her legs looked fragile — even in death, with a heavy bruise on the ankle. Her hands hung limply by her side with rips of flesh in her finger-nails. Flies buzzed around the body.

Baba's eyes flirted to the hockey-stick beside the body. It was coated with blood and bits of bone. One daring fly perched on the mouth of the corpse and began to move delicately. It was almost as if the thing was waltzing. Without warning it suddenly flew straight for the detective. Baba ducked, then made a sign to Jumbo to cover the body again.

Jumbo regarded him questioningly as they moved away from the body.

"Well?"

"A cold-blooded murder." Baba said with feeling. He knew her in the police force though they had seldom spoken to each other. The reason being that he hated her the way he hated all ugly women. Not that she'd done him anything. But being ugly. Bah! She aroused the same revulsion in him which usually resulted in hatred.

"Where did she die?" He asked Jumbo.

"Over there."

"How about you John? What's your verdict about the cause of death?"

The doctor's good-natured fat face split into a grin. "It's there for all to see. Someone delivered a fearsome blow on the base of her skull with that hockey-stick. All those rips of flesh on her nails are strong pointers to the fact that there must have been a struggle.

Probably the guy at first planned to strangle her — there are nail marks on her throat; then she got too tough for him and he hit her with the hockey-stick. I could have a more positive result after the post-mortem."

"Let's go to the exact spot where the body was found. I'd like an inspection."

With Jumbo leading the way into the alley, they picked their way carefully. After they'd walked for some metres, the sergeant suddenly pointed to a big boulder.

"That's where her body was found. In the space between that rock and the wall."

Baba walked forward to the rock, squatted down beside it and inspected the place where the body had been found. Dry blood clung to the underside of the rock and some of the sand there were also coated in red. Peering at the ground more closely he suddenly discovered a thin, steady line of coagulated blood in the sand. Following the line closely, he found himself walking towards the centre of the alley. He came to an abrupt stop and motioned with his hand for the others to join him.

It was apparent that the earth had been disturbed here. There were the distinct sign of a struggle — with the imprints of feet left carelessly. A few metres away from these imprints lay more caked-blood, bits of bone and brain. He peered at the ground more closely, feeling a thrill run through him. This was where the murder had been committed. It was likely that not many people had passed here since last night — for though there were a lot of other foot-prints, most didn't look as bold and recent as these ones.

He got up slowly, stared at the two men with him, and pointed to the ground.

"That's where she was knocked off."

Immediately the two men squatted to peer at the ground closely. The doctor was the first to get up.

"You're right." He said slowly. "That part of the sand which was disturbed points to my theory of a struggle."

Baba glanced at his watch. It was late morning.

"I'd like a very comprehensive report as quick as possible, John. Don't forget to find out the blood-group of the owner of those rips of flesh on her nails." He grinned at the doctor. "This is right up your alley. I guess you'll have to come up with something that I could use."

A pause, then he wrinkled his nose. "Let's get out of this damned alley."

As they began plodding towards the exit, the detective turned to Jumbo.

"Any witnesses to the murder?"

"None yet. But we haven't interviewed them."

"The fingerprint guys worked on the body yet?"

He lifted his shoulders helplessly. "Nothing yet but they've just started. I told them to work on the hands and legs first so that we could get the body out of the alley."

Baba considered this for a moment.

"Okay get the fingerprint experts to finish their job on the body so that John can have it quickly. About those foot-prints in the alley — you're an experienced guy so I don't have to tell you they're vitally important. Get those experts cracking there too and keep off the crowd until they finish." He paused to recollect his breath. "I'm going to be busy for some time so you'll continue handling this show until I'm ready to take over. Go over that alley with a tooth-comb. We mustn't miss anything. You'll also have to give it to the neighbours — one of them might have seen or heard something.

"Know where she lives?" He asked suddenly.

Jumbo pointed to a house not far from the alley. "That's her place."

"I'm going there now to conduct a hurried search of the place. I won't disturb things. I also want you to go over that house later with a tooth-comb. Leave nothing unchecked." He stopped to glance at his watch again, then patted the guy on his shoulders. "I'll see you sometime in the afternoon or evening."

The crowd parted to allow him pass. Getting into his squad car, he drove over to the house. The door to the sitting room was open and he entered warily. He glanced around, noting how poorly she had lived. She used the sitting room as a bedroom also. Going over to a small table he picked up an album and began leafing through it. There weren't many men in the album — not that he'd expected to find many. He was interested mainly in the men — the girls and old folk he merely gave casual glances. There was just that possibility that her killer was acquainted with her. He went through a collection of more pictures — again finding men rare.

Pulling out a drawer on the table beside the bed, he began going over the contents. He came upon some of her mail. She had few mail and most were from old, uninteresting people. Bah! This muck-suckle woman must have lived one of the dreariest lives he'd ever seen. With some cynicism he realized that the guy who knocked her off might have done her good justice. By the time he had gone over her suitcase, he found himself hating her more and more.

The trouble was that for people who lived like that, whenever any of them got murdered, it was always irritating trying to develop a lead for usually there was so little to go on.

Finally he checked the kitchen in a hurry and not finding anything of value to him left — carrying her pictures and mail and cursing vehemently. He'd go over those items more carefully later.

On the way to the bank he stopped at a restaurant where he had a big lunch — for he hadn't eaten in the morning. Then he drove over to the bank. Parking the car near the entrance to the bank, he got out and walked to the bank and paused before one of the cashiers and flashed his badge.

"Where's the Financial Manager?" He asked, noting that there were few customers in the bank.

The cashier eyed him up and down then pointed to a man who sat behind a cabinet desk, away from the others — with two telephones and a pile of papers on his desk. As Baba crossed into the workers' territory and began walking towards him, he noticed that the guy's hands were shaking. He stopped in front of the man's desk and flashed his badge.

"Detective Omo Baba. Police Headquarters."

The Financial Manager regarded him with an apprehensive look, then waved him to one of the chairs opposite him. He wrung his hands together as Baba sat down.

"What can I do for you? You've come about last night's robbery, I guess?"

Baba nodded. "I'll be glad if you'd be helpful to us in answering a few questions. We've already met the General Manager this morning and he's given us the go-ahead."

"Go on. This robbery has been a terrible blow on all of us. I'll be glad to help in any way."

Baba produced his notebook and pen, scribbled down something then looked up.

"Name?" He asked.

"Ray Atu."

"You work at the Bendel State Bank?"

"Yeah."

"Post?"

"Financial Manager."

"You know the guys who robbed this bank?"

"Of course not!" The Financial Manager shouted indignantly, his eyes glowering.

"I'm sorry. Didn't mean to upset you. Just routine questioning." He paused until the Manager's eyes had shed their light, then stabbed on. "You think this robbery is an internal job?"

The guy shrugged non-committally. "Could be, though one can't be too sure. I think this bank has got one of the best security systems in the country. It's almost fool-proof. I guess anyone who who robs it must have had an inside accomplice."

"There are a lot of guys working in the bank. Do you suspect any of them to be shady? Any of them with a record?"

Atu thought for a moment, then shook his head.

"Don't think any of them has a record. We don't employ guys with records. If any of them is shady then he's been camouflaging it."

Baba tried another angle.

"You just said your security system is 'almost' fool-proof. What makes you think so?"

"You mean you don't know anything about our security arrangements?" Atu countered.

"I know all that. What I'm asking is what makes you think the security arrangements are 'almost' fool-proof?"

"Aw, that's simple. No one can rob that bank without the keys.

You probably know that. Next, a rogue couldn't possibly get near the bank doors without first putting the guards out of action. It's almost but not fool-proof. Fool-proof against a guy who doesn't know about the security arrangements. It will take a guy who is familiar with the arrangements before the system becomes almost fool-proof."

"You heard that the robbers drugged the guards' supper."

"Did they?"

"You mean you haven't heard?"

"I've heard. But it hadn't been identified as happened through their supper."

"Yeah; that supper they usually have at eight was doped by the robbers."

"A clever move on their part."

Baba felt that suffocating rage in his chest but he quickly smothered it.

"Doesn't it occur to you that this supper thing is absurd?" He queried. "You ever heard of bank guards being allowed officially to take supper while on duty? You ever heard about that happening elsewhere in the whole world?"

"This is different. It arose out of necessity."

"How?" Baba asked. He had that instinctive nose for something fishy. And once he'd smelled something he'd keep hammering at the point.

"One of the guards was reported wandering around one day, looking for something to eat. So the former General Manager raised it at a Board meeting and suggested this supper thing as a counter-measure to combat this wandering for food. It was adopted by the Board."

"You said the former General Manager?"

"Yes. No longer works here. Was . . . . ." Atu frowned, then his eyes opened wide and he began to tremble slightly.

Looking at him closely, Baba instinctively knew that a nickel had dropped in the guy's mind — that this could be the break he'd been praying for. Unconsciously he pulled his chair closer, then his tone softened to confidential.

"What have you remembered, Ray?"

"Off the record?"

"Yeah. Count on me any day. This is off the record."

The Financial Manager leaned closer on the desk, his eyes sparkling.

"Know what I think? If anyone organised that robbery, then it's the former General Manager."

"What makes you think so?"

"I didn't remember him before. That guy's got a reputation for shady deals. Got retired by the Federal Government in 1975 for misappropriation of funds." He paused, then rattled on. "On the day of this Board meeting I spoke of — that is when this supper thing was being debated, he was so anxious that the suggestion should be adopted."

"What's his name?"

"Brian Obi."

"Address."

"8 Ajobi Road. You paying him a visit?"

Baba nodded. "Any other information you can give me?"

Atu shook his head then stared at Baba. "Better be careful of that guy. If he thought for a second you had him cornered, he might do something nasty."

The detective's grin was confident. "Don't worry about that. Two can always play dirty. I've handled tougher guys before."

"Maybe, but be careful."

"Thanks. I'll be."

He was about to get up when one of the clerks who'd been hovering nearby walked to the desk and dumped a sheaf of papers in front of Atu. There were worried lines on his forehead.

"These papers are for Mr. Buko, sir." He said. "He hasn't arrived up till now. I thought you'd decide to sign them as they're holding up some payments."

"What!" Atu was beside himself with rage as he glanced at his watch. "It's already afternoon. You mean he hasn't come to work!"

"Could be sir. I haven't seen him all day and his chair has been empty."

Baba's sharp mind had latched into this new development like a leech. He could feel the bells of expectation jangling inside him.

He raised his forefinger to signal an interruption.

"What's the name of the guy you're talking about?"

Atu looked slightly impatient as he waved his hands. "Why do you ask? Think this could be a lead?"

"It's my job to ask questions. A good cop has got to snoop into anything that smells."

"Well if you insist. His name's Mike Buko. He's the Assistant Financial Manager — my deputy. If you think he'd something to do with last night's robbery then you're onto a wild goose-chase. That guy's no robber. It's just mere coincidence that he's not around this morning."

"We'll see." Baba said thoughtfully. On a sudden hunch, he asked! "Has he ever failed to come to work before?"

"No. This is the first time. But as I said before, mere coincidence."

"Do you think he has been having money problems of late?"

"Can't say for sure. He's planning to get married next month . . . . should be a very expensive wedding. If he was having money problems, he wouldn't be planning such an expensive wedding."

"Know the name of his fiancee?"

"Pat Ola."

"Ever seen her?"

Atu nodded.

"Describe her."

"Small, dark, lithe with heavy breasts. Smashing, if you know what I mean."

"Where does Buko live?"

Atu thought for some time. To his annoyance he found he'd forgotten Buko's address. Maybe it was this endless, killing bank job that made him forget some trivial things easily.

The clerk who'd been standing, listening open-mouthed to the interrogation now spoke.

"I remember his address sir."

"What's it chap?" Baba asked.

"10 Oba square." The clerk replied, looking nervously at his boss to see whether he approved.

"Go on Bob. Tell him anything he wants." Atu said re-assuringly.

"He'll need every co-operation if he's going to catch these robbers."

Bolder now, the clerk held his shoulders high and stared at Baba intelligently. "I've something important I'll like to say."

"Shoot." The detective said, feeling sweat running on his palm.

"Yesterday, when I brought some papers to Mr. Buko to sign, he started grumbling. Said that the only thing one did at the bank is to work. In other words he started raving. Said that the bank expects one to work himself to death for peanuts. He swore that he wouldn't work here again after today. "Why should I work here when I'm coming into the big money?"

"You sure he said that?" Baba couldn't hide the excitement as he watched the guy closely.

"Positive. He was talking like someone in a dream. I couldn't have been surer."

The detective heaved a long drawn breath of relief. "What's your personal opinion about him? Think he could have gone to the extent of planning to rob a bank?"

Again the clerk glanced at his boss who nodded his go-ahead.

"Mr. Buko's proud as a peacock and very loquacious but herein lies the stunt. I think he's too proud to condescend to robbery and more over he hasn't got the guts. One can't be too sure he didn't know about it judging from those words of his. But it's only one chance in five that he's involved."

Baba nodded grimly. He didn't like this line so much. He tried another gambit.

"Was there anything he said or did yesterday that you considered out of the ordinary?"

"Wait a minute!" Atu interrupted sharply. He lifted a file from his desk, leafed through the pages until he came to the page he wanted. He glanced at the contents for a moment, a frown on his face. "Buko yesterday wanted to help secure a loan for one Charles Okala, Director of Okala Transport Company Ltd. The documents required for the loan were incomplete so I told him to wait until today. When later I stumbled on the list of registered companies, this one wasn't there. Something looked phoney about the loan . . . . incomplete documents and the rush. I was planning to querry Mike this morning before this robbery thing happened."

Baba closed his notebook and got up slowly. "Thanks a lot for the cooperation, Mr. Atu. I think my time here was well spent. I'll be back if I need more clarification." He winked at the clerk and began treading his way out of the bank. He seemed to be walking on air. This was one of the most lucky breaks he'd ever had in his history as a detective officer. Though he'd been praying inwardly for a break, this was simply unexpected and it swept him off his feet completely.

In his little notebook were two suspects who might have acted as inside help. He felt sure that it had to be one of them — the two just couldn't miss. If his instinct was right, then these two guys were somehow involved — not only one of them. He never doubted for a moment the fame it will bring him if he busted this case — plus ten thousand.

Ten thousand! The re-collection of that reward made him quicken his race. Once outside the bank he raced towards his squad car.

B

Jimoh held his breath for a moment as the knocking persisted, then motioning to the others to wait, he tip-toed into the sitting room, parted the curtains and peered outside. Not seeing any police vehicle hanging around, he released his breath and walking quickly to the door, opened it. The members of the gang had quickly submerged their hostilities for the moment in readiness to face a common enemy — if it was an enemy knocking on the door.

At the door stood the land-lady of the apartment.

"I've been knocking for ages." She said with reproach in her eyes. "Why didn't you open quickly?"

Jimoh switched on his charm. "Aw, hello Madam. Do come in please." He made way, ushering her in with a wave of his hand. As she entered, he said. "I'm sorry to have kept you waiting. I was busy. Maybe that's why I didn't hear the knocking for some time."

She sat down in one of the easy chairs and drew her legs together. Her eyes took in the room with one sweeping glance. She clucked in her throat.

"The furniture and decorations fair." She said reluctantly. "Not bad for a man. But it still needs a woman's touch. A home's never very nice without a woman to fuss over it."

Jimoh's smile widened. "I can take care of an apartment better than a woman." He switched on the radio. "What will you take?"

"Malt."

Going over to the refrigerator he picked up a bottle of malt, a glass and opener, then glanced into the room where the rest of the gang were.

"It's the land-lady." He said in hushed tones. "You can come out."

He opened the drink and dumped it with the glass beside her just as Puna and the other members of the gang filed into the room. She raised a questioning eyebrow at him.

"My friends." He said, indicating with his hand. "Joe. Ify. Bill." Pausing theatrically to allow a moment of suspense then, "hi chaps, meet the land-lady of the house. Mrs. Amin."

The guys murmured their welcome.

"Glad to know your friends. They all look like nice folk."

Jimoh grinned agreeably. "Couldn't find nicer folks elsewhere."

Just then there was an interruption of the normal music programme and the announcer's voice came on the line — clear and feminine:

'Here is an important announcement. With reference to last night's robbery at the Bendel State Bank, the Police Commissioner implores all and sundry who may have relevant information regarding that robbery to come foward to the Police and render their information. A reward of two thousand naira awaits anyone who renders very useful information. Also anyone who gives information leading directly to the arrest of the robbers will get a reward of ten thousand naira. The Police commissioner went further to warn that any person withholding information is doing so at his or her own risk and doing a disservice to himself and his nation. He advises all to report any suspicious characters to the police. Finally he gives an assurance that the police is leaving no stone unturned to track down these robbers and hinted that arrests could be likely soon.'

Unconsciously all the members of the gang had been holding their breaths. Now they breathed down more easily. Looking at them the land-lady had an uneasy feeling that something was wrong. However, Jimoh, the charming Stage Manager, was quick to the situation.

"You heard about the robbery?" He asked.

She nodded. "It's the talk of the town. The general concensus is that the robbers are pretty smart guys though I don't think so. If they were smart, one of them couldn't have gotten himself killed."

"Could be the one who got himself killed was dumb." Jimoh offered.

"Maybe. But if they were pretty smart they wouldn't have taken him along for a job like that."

Jimoh shrugged in mock nonchalance. "What's it to me anyway. There are times when I think the whole lousy cops we have in this City are mugs. If they have one of the robbers, albeit it dead, all they have to do is use him in tracing the rest."

She finished her drink and got up. "I'd like to check the garage."

"What?" It was out before Jimoh could control himself and there was a sharp edge to it.

"The garage." She said, looking at him curiously. "What's wrong with my wanting to check the garage?"

"Nothing." He said crisply, feeling sweat running down his armpit. Those two corpses, Kpondo and Buko, were still inside the ambulance in the garage. He was sure that once she saw the ambulance, her sharp brain would put one and one together and get two. Knowing how obstinate she could be, he figured he's require all his wile to dissuade her from continued insistence. "Looking for something in the garage?"

She nodded. "My ring. I removed it from my finger and kept it on the floor when I wanted to carry out some things from the garage yesterday. Forgot to take it later. Should be there now."

"Oh, I'm awfully sorry. When I swept there this morning I didn't see any ring. Either someone else took it or I swept it away unknowingly."

For a moment her cheeks sagged with disappointment, then she said hopefully. "Don't worry about it. If it's lost, it's lost. But it could still be there. I'll check."

Jimoh drew in his breath slowly. His heart was thudding dully as he glanced casually at his accomplices. They looked apprehensive. He decided to try an ace.

"I don't know what you'll think of me but what ever you think I guess you're justified." He faked a very sober 'I wouldn't do it again' look. "I don't know where I kept the key after sweeping the garage. I've been looking for it since. I'm positive it's somewhere in the house. It'll probably take me a day or two to find it."

His sober-repentant look made her swallow her distaste. "Aw, that's all right. This is not something you should start falling on your knees for I've got a duplicate key here." She walked to the door and opened it. "I'll be back in a minute. All I want is to make sure." Then she was outside.

For a moment Jimoh closed his eyes, a vein pounding on his forehead. When he opened his eyes a marked change had come over him. He was now back to a killer. Once she'd seen inside that garage he was going to kill. Quickly he strode outside.

She was fumbling with the key in the lock as he approached her. His fists were clenched as he came to stand beside her, his heart-beats accelerating startlingly. Wiping the sweat from his eyes he brought up his hands slowly. Suddenly she cried out.

"Hey. What's this?" She stopped and picked up a torquoise ring. Jimoh relaxed his bunched-up muscles.

Balancing it in her finger, she glanced over her shoulder at him and smiled. "Isn't it beautiful?" She purred, unaware of how close death had been.

"Sure." Jimoh said in a strangled voice. "The ring is smashing. Would like to get one like that for my girl friend."

As she slipped the ring on her finger, the eunuch leaned on the garage door. "How is your husband? I guess he's getting on fine with his work."

She gave an imperceptible nod, then glanced at her watch. "Good gracious!" She exclaimed. "He should be back by now. I'd better run along to prepare his lunch." She withdrew her key, waved a bye-bye at him and hurried down the road to where she'd parked her car.

The others were just coming out as she hurried away. "What happened?" Young asked.

"She found her ring just in time. I could have wrung her neck if she'd looked into that garage." He tried the garage door, found it was still locked and started going back into the house. He was followed closely by Ify and Young but Puna stayed outside.

Ify and Young went up to Young's room which by mutual though silent agreement was now for the two of them.

"I'm getting scared, Bill." She said as he secured the bolt in place. "Seems a violent showdown will take place soon over the splitting of this money. Don't you think we could end up getting nothing?"

"Don't worry about that, baby. We've earned our share so no bum is gypping us out of it. I shoot fast. Any guy who tries it will have to shoot faster." He led her towards the bed. "With me around you needn't be scared baby. I'll get that gun from Joe when he's off guard."

"But the police Bill . . . . you heard the announcement?"

He patted her flank and drew her down on the bed. "You worry too much babe. The police play a psychological game. Too much noise and little action. That's one of their gambits — to stampede us into running scared in circles."

He nuzzled her cheeks then regarded her admiringly. The naked desire in her eyes made him grab her savagely. He found her lips, unbuttoned them and began drenching her with hot searing kisses. Her response was quick — full of experience and adventure. She moaned in her throat as their tongues met — an exquisite moan that made him want her more.

He paused to regain the breath that was rattling in his throat when she pushed him away impatiently and started to undress. Swearing in his throat he began throwing off his clothes and it turned into a race of who would finish first. As she threw off her blouse, her breasts bubbled into view. He paused in his undressing to gape at her, feeling his mouth water at the sight of those luscious ripe breasts. She wore silk panties of the most alluring blue. He raised some fingers towards one of her breasts but she struck his hand away.

Looking at him coyly, Ify's hands hovered on the elastic band of her panties. Then she dragged them off under his lusting gaze. So she beat him in the race to undress, with minutes to spare but he didn't care. He was busy staring at her ravishing body.

Her body was the colour of flowing brass, a colour that never failed to captivate him. She had large, firm breasts that stood out like beckoning ripe pawpaw. The nipples stood erect and defiant with roseates that alternated between a captivating brass and a tantalising faint-red.

Slowly his eyes moved down to a flat-torso that held more than promise for him. The hips were firmly athletic and curved — curved and large enough to make his fingers itch to explore.

She lay back on the bed and watched him admire her, then she said in a very soft sexy voice. "Come to me Billy boy."

He wasn't finished with her yet. She was so much of a contrast to Bisi Eyo — whom he had murdered. He had the feeling that if he'd seen Ify naked sooner than this, he might have killed Joe.

She had slim, nice legs that enlarged to form rippling thighs. At the junction of her things was the gateway to ecstasy. His mouth opened in wonder and desire at the sight of the small, wet pussy that was pulsating with life. The hairs here were simply copper-brown, ringing the mounds of venus that jealously guarded their precious gateway.

He went beserk for an instant. Tearing his clothes off in a frenzy, he jumped on top of her, grabbing her savagely and not letting her go. She struggled against his superior strength, gasping and choking for he was suffocating her. When he regained his reason he became aware that her fingers were tracing intricate patterns on his hard arse.

Finding one of her nipples with his lips he began to suck it tantalisingly with almost baby-like greed, while one of his hands played with the other nipple. He could feel the nipples harden — one straining inside his mouth while she squirmed under him.

She grabbed his startling piston of manhood and pushed him off her so that she could see it more. She toyed with it — weighing it in her palm, using her expert fingers to discover the promise it held

for her. The effect was stimulating. Her eyes grew wide as saucers —
with a mixture of awe and startled curiousity as that piece of manhood grew to fearful proportions. It was now a turgid, thumping
cock that was stubborn with passion and which showed no sign of
budging until it had satisfied its immediate desire.

Mechanically her legs parted. "Now. Now." She moaned in her
throat. "I want it now."

Slowly, almost theatrically, the cock came into her, feeling its
way in unknown terrain. Then she felt it rise and pound away, rise
and pound away. On the third stroke she rose up to meet him,
then began to set a tempo of her own — a tempo that was both fast
and demanding. He matched her tempo for tempo, merging with
her whenever they met and hearing little-girl cries in her throat.

She moaned, gasped, clawed at him and bit him as he ravaged her.
She was good and strong and gave as much as she received. Her
moans were a source of delight to him — whenever she moaned he
jabbed harder. It was a long time in coming — but it started as a
heat in his loins. Gradually it changed to a burning liquid fire. He
could feel the rumble in him and she sensed it before the explosion
— the explosion of all the tension they had had to bear since they
robbed the Bendel State Bank. Her orgasm came at the same time
as his and they exploded together in space. Her eyes rolled back and
even her last cry of pleasure, "Bill . . . . Billy . . . . ." was lost in
the sharp descent into oblivion.

VIII

A

Baba leaned against the door, his eyes skinned for trouble as he listened for any sound inside the house. A grand-father clock chimed four times. The beating of his heart was slightly faster than normal. For a slight reassurance he glanced at the two policemen standing on opposite sides of him, their guns trained on the door.

Not hearing any sound he knocked on the door three times and waited, his hand on the butt of the .45 automatic he carried inside the leather holster around his waist. To his annoyance he noticed that he was sweating and to keep up his spirits, he tried to convince himself that it was the thought of the reward which made him sweat. He just couldn't be scared of a former General Manager of a bank who should be ageing and slow. Slightly impatient and edgy, he banged on the door this time, standing away from the key-hole so that anyone peering through it wouldn't see him.

He waited for two more minutes and when nothing happened, he lost his patience. He tried the door and found it locked. Moving back a step he beckoned to one of the policemen who quickly sidled over to his side. Baba withdrew the gun grom its holster and released the safety catch.

"When I count up to three, we ram the door." He whispered to the cop. He had specially brought them along in case the game turned dirty. "Better be at full alert. He could be waiting behind the door with a sub-machine gun. Ready?" It was a long time ago when he vowed never to offer himself for target-practice.

The cop nodded. The other cop covered them from behind.

"One." He counted. "Two . . . . three." They slammed into the door with the full strength of their shoulders. The door quivered under the impact, then flew inwards violently. The two of them were propelled half-way into the sitting room by the remaining force of their charge. Baba twisted himself, then spun around in a crouch, the .45 ready for action.

To his utter disappointment, it was an empty room that the blunt-nose of the .45 stared at. Moving warily, he entered the nearest bedroom, the gun poised but this also harboured no Brian Obi. By the time he had gone over the elegantly furnished apartment he was fit to hit the ceiling. His first thought was that the guy might have seen them coming and fled through a back exit. But as he came back into the sitting room he noticed one of the cops holding up an ash-tray with stale ash and cigarette butts in it. It was then he realized that the air in the apartment was stale — the house hadn't been swept this morning.

Figuring that no one had been inside this apartment for some time, probably a day, he stationed the guards at the door. He wasn't taking any chances. Though without a search warrant, he was confident Ogunbor will see him safe any day if court-action was taken against him.

Methodically he began going through drawers, shelves, flipping through huge volumes of books on Management, Banking and bla bla. He didn't really know what he was looking for — but his instincts told him he could find something incriminating . . . . a sketch of the bank, a letter . . . . something. At the end of an hour and half he had gone over virtually every scrap of paper in the house, the wardrobes, suitcases, diaries, *et cetera*. By the time he finished, his earlier euphoria had evaporated. Maybe he'd underrated this Obi guy. Could be the guy was more uncanny than he had thought.

Just at that moment the policeman he had left to take care of the squad car barged into the room, panting from the exertion of running up the stairs. Baba who was already spinning around, his gun ready for action, checked himself.

"Something wrong?" He asked the policeman.

"The Chief wants you at headquarters right away. Says something has turned up."

Baba's mind raced very quickly. He lifted one of the portraits on the wall — he guessed this was Brian Obi. Carrying the portrait, he stopped at the door.

"When I've gone, you guys should leave this apartment." He instructed the two cops standing at the door. "Close the door after you but don't go far. Stick around the neighbourhood. If you spot any character coming into the apartment or the ex-Bank Manager I told you about, bring him or her back to headquarters for questioning. I'll be contacting you guys soon. I have to rush to headquarters." Still carrying the portrait, he left the apartment at a run, took the stairs four at a time and sprinted towards their car parked some metres away.

Fifteen minutes later he was ascending the stairs to his Chief's office. He shoved his way past an excited Okuns and barged into Ogunbor's office.

Ogunbor was pacing up and down the office, one hand in pocket and smoking a pipe feverishly. At the sound of the door opening, he pivotted on his heels and his eyes fell on Baba.

"You're quick." He said flatly and began walking back towards his desk. "All this time we had a General prize in our hands and we didn't know it."

Baba started for a moment then his ears began to itch. "What's the gigantic prize? The robbers have been nabbed?"

"Somehow." The police chief said evasively then staring at Baba levelly across the desk he said. "That robber who committed suicide has been identified. He is the former Seneral Manager of Bendel State Bank."

Baba sucked in his breath sharply. Though he'd been almost cock-sure that Obi had something to do with that robbery, he hadn't been working on the theory that the ex-Manager took part in the actual robbing of the bank. To think that the man he was looking for was the one that had gotten killed in the operation — the corpse that had been in their hands all along, was ironic if not frustrating. Ironic in that he had been seeking miles away for somebody in his laps; albeit a corpse. Frustrating in that now his hopes of nabbing the ex-Manager and wringing information from him were now dashed to the rocks. Then he remembered he still had an ace, there was Mike Buko. Yeala! Mike Buko! The last ace he had for the meantime. And deadly! Yeah, he was determined to make it count.

"What are you thinking for hell's sake?" Ogunbor demanded, an impatient note in his voice. The Commissioner of Police had literally taken him apart and this roasting put him in no mood for patience.

Baba shrugged as usual. "Makes little difference now — his identification."

The Chief's jowls expanded in smothered rage as he hovered at the verge of a volcanic eruption. "What do you mean it makes little difference? You've been in this case since morning and you haven't been able to establish a lead on these robbers. Then when someone identifies the corpse on our hands and gives us a worthy lead, you say it makes no difference. Don't you see that if we search his place we might find something."

This time Baba camouflaged a superior smile by yawning. "I've searched his place. I didn't find ...." He remembered he'd forgotten the portrait of Obi in the squad car. "The only thing of value I laid my hands on was his portrait."

There was slight disbelief in Ogunbor's eyes. "You mean you've been to Brian Obi's house?"

Baba nodded. "You were still at the meeting when I came around. I took two of our men and broke into his apartment."

"And you didn't find anything?" Ogunbor asked as if he didn't hear the first time.

"His portrait. Nothing else."

The Chief sank into his chair wearily. "How did you find out about Obi's complicity in the robbery?"

"I interrogated some chaps at the bank. One of them felt the ex-Manager had something to do with the robbery. Said the Manager had pulled off shady deals in the past and was booted out of the bank by the Federal Government for misappropriation of funds. What ......"

"So you acted on the hunch?" He interrupted.

"Sort of." Baba replied. "You know, all that bit about serving supper to the guards at the bank made me suspicious. It just isn't the practice the world over. I was convinced that this not only presented a security lapse but made it damn too easy to rob the bank. The whole thing was just like taking sweets from a kid. When this bank chap said it was Obi who had suggested it while he was the Bank Manager I was almost certain I had my man."

The Chief allowed him a passing smile. "That was clever of you." He paused. "That reminds me. Did you get anything from Miss Eyo's angle? Any lead there?"

"Little. The best we could get was the killer's footprints. I'll start investigating the robbery from her angle once I exhaust my present avenue. For the moment I've assigned Phil to be handling that angle."

The look on the chief's face was despairing. "First it was Tim Aina. Then a bank robbery with a string of deaths attached. Miss Eyo knocked off. One guard at the bank killed. Then to rub salt on injury three of my men shot down. And all we can show for our efforts is one of their gang dead and no lead to them. At this rate this city will crumble in no time."

"I've still got a deadly ace left." Baba said quickly.

"Then what is it? Damn you, spill it out. The Commissioner sits in his office screaming his fat arse off for action and here you are playing a cagey game with me."

Baba was slightly shocked. He had never suspected that his Chief could vomit such venom. Maybe it was the direction in which the city was heading. For a Chief of Police to be watching almost helplessly as his city became a playground for criminals was shattering. It was enough to drive even a strong-nerved guy nuts.

Feeling almost sorry for Ogunbor he laid his notebook in front of him. "It's all in there."

Ogunbor snatched up the notebook the way a hawk snatches a chick, and began to read greedily. His face was expressionless as he read, then suddenly his countenance changed as he came to the bit about Mike Buko. He read it slowly but breathlessly and when he finished, his mouth curled into a smile. For a fleeting second, the shadows under his eyes disappeared and his jowls radiated freshness.

"What are we waiting for?" He demanded crisply as he got up

from his chair. "This could be it. As far as I'm concerned there's no better lead than this at the moment." He paused to jerk out a drawer and take his gun. Fitting it into the leather holster around his waist, he said to the detective: "I'm coming along in this operation. Go and get ready two squad cars and round up some of the boys. They should be armed to the teeth."

As the detective ran out, Ogunbor entered his secretary's office and stopped to glance at his watch. 6.01.

"Take care of the office." He said. "It's action time. I'll be back soon."

Moving sprightly for a man of his bulk, he bumped into Doctor Moziah as he left the room. The doctor looked surprised at seeing Ogunbor moving with so much haste.

"What's it for hell's sake?" Ogunbor demanded as he tried to shove the doc out of the way.

Moziah stood his ground and held up a sheaf of papers he was carrying. "The results of the tests I've been carrying out." He said.

Ogunbor took the papers and patted him on the shoulders. "I know you must have done a good job. I'm in a hurry now. I'll call on you later when I've had time to read the report."

Carrying the sheaf of papers with him, he ran down the stairs.

Ten minutes later, their patrol car was speeding along Ring Road, closely followed by another patrol car filled with sharp-shooters of the Nigerian Police Force, Benin City branch. The leading vehicle turned into Mission Road and the second patrol car followed suit.

Ogunbor sat at the back of the leading patrol car, his head bowed over the report he was holding. To his irritation he found he couldn't concentrate on it; his mind was too occupied with this lead they were following. Impatiently he flung the report on the seat beside him and stared out through the window.

This was the rush hour just before darkness fell. Inhabitants of the city were hurrying helter-skelter, not wanting to reach home after dark. Thinking wryly that all these tension and macabre events of the past few days had made an insignificant impact on the life of the city, he shifted his eyes to where they were going.

Baba sat in the front beside the drivers, staring through the rear-view mirror. He had been observing his boss worriedly for sometime. He could tell whenever a man was soaked to the teeth with tension. All of them were soaked with tension — who wouldn't be when they knew the sort of enemy they were going to face. But he knew that his boss was the most strung up of the lot. For two nights running he had barely had a wink of sleep — starting from the time Aina had been murdered. In a way Baba figured that the earlier the climax the better. If this thing dragged on for much longer, someone was going to break down.

Just then the driver brought the patrol car to a halt in front of 6 Oba square, two blocks away from 10 Oba square where Buko lived. The second patrol car pulled up behind them.

Getting out of the car, Ogunbor and Baba went the few remaining metres on foot with the rest of the party keeping a safe distance behind. Ogunbor surveyed the apartment. The house was in darkness for night had come and he had the despairing feeling that there was no one inside the house.

Nevertheless he motioned to four of the sharpshooters who quickly took up positions around the house as he had briefed them at Headquarters. Then Baba and two other policemen approached the house cautiously. As they mounted the stairs, Baba cocked the hammer of his gun. At the balcony he paused to glance back. He couldn't see Ogunbor but he knew the Chief was squatting against the wall of the house.

Lifting his hands he knocked loudly. The seconds ticked away but there was no response. This time he banged on the door. Listening to the frightening silence around the house he had the feeling that this was following the pattern of his last escapade. A little impatient he signalled to the two cops with him. Turning the knob he found the door locked. Coming at the door they battered it down and burst into the room. The stale air told him the whole story. Snapping on the lights he called out to Ogunbor who joined him with some of the sharpshooters in no time.

They went over the apartment carefully, searching despairingly for any clue but found nothing. At the end of it Ogunbor's jowls became more shrunken. He was ready to collapse any minute. The fatigue showed in his eyes.

Then suddenly Baba who had been poking inside a dust bin gave an excited cry. "Hey! what's this?" A note. On the note was written Charles Okala, 4B Woods Avenue.

"We're coming nearer home." He squealed.

IX

A

Puna put his ear to the key-hole and listened carefully. The only sound he could hear was the snoring of the eunuch. He peeped through the key-hole but he couldn't see anything for the room was in total darkness. Satisfied that the eunuch was asleep he now deemed it safe to carry out the plan he had in mind — a plan he had nearly botched in the afternoon. A few minutes ago he had checked up Ify's bedroom and discovered to his immense satisfaction that the two new lovers were asleep in each other's arms.

His heart beating slightly he tiptoed to the door leading into the room where all the money was stored. Inserting the key in the lock he cautiously pushed back the door. It gave a sharp creak as it opened and for a moment Puna stood rooted to the spot, his heart in his mouth. Then moving like lightning he quickly hid behind the door and drew out the .38 from his pocket waiting for the eunuch's door to open. After two minutes and the door didn't open, he came out from hiding.

He lifted one of the crates — the biggest and carrying it, left the room. He was sweating as he carried the crate past the sitting room and into the cool night. The garage door was open, the light on, for he had been into it before and shifted the bodies. The decomposing bodies were now at one end of the garage and the whole place stank. He wrinkled his nose in disgust as he dumped the crate inside the ambulance. Moving quickly, he repeated his trip. On the fourth trip he peeped again through the key-hole into Jimoh's room. He found the room still in darkness and snoring sounds still coming from inside the room. Grinning and more confident now he continued his task. By the time he dumped the sixth crate in the back of the ambulance he was fagged out. He decided to leave the seventh crate for them reckoning they would need money to keep out of police trouble.

Checking his pocket he reassured himself that the car keys were still there. Now he was going to carry out the most tricky part of his plan. Since the bank robbery Joe had spent almost every hour with Pat Ola for he was crazy about her. Even this daring plan of his was being undertaken because he wanted to take her to a faraway place where he could give all his attention to her. Though she was stunning, more beautiful than Ify, what Puna adored most about her was her class. He was obsessed with beautiful dames of class.

Once back in the passage, he locked the door to where the remaining crate was. When they discovered him missing, they would break down the door. He opened the door to the bedroom he shared with Pat — though he still kept her tied at times for fear of her running away, and his hand paused on the knob.

Tip-toeing to the eunuch's room again he peered through the key-hole. A powerful jolt ran through him. The light in Jimoh's bedroom was now on! Feeling his heart thumping and a hairy hand snaking up his spine, he tried the knob and the door opened silently. With one hand on his gun-butt he entered the room. And received a more powerful jolt! Jimoh was nowhere in the room! Scared and nervous, with sweat running down his back he drew out the gun, telling himself he was the only guy who had a gun. Jimoh couldn't have any. Yet for some inexplicable reason he felt scared.

Gun in hand he moved out into the passage. The passage was still empty so he went back to his room. Still holding the gun he proceeded to unlace the silk stockings he'd used in tying her before. Her face was pale and she looked sickly as she'd done since the killing of her fiancé.

Supporting her with one hand while the other hand held the gun he led her out of the room, his eyes very alert. He wasn't playing the cool game any longer. Being the only guy with a gun he had decided to come out into the open. No one dared challenge him empty-handed — even for all that money.

Her feet making shuffling noises on the floor they moved out of the sitting room, past the verandah and into the garage. He paused inside the garage, glancing around warily to make sure Gilt wasn't there. Convinced, he led her to the front of the ambulance, opened the door to the passengers' side and pushed her in and closed the door. Moving to the back of the ambulance he closed the door too.

Then the light in the garage went out! Joe's heart bumped violently and began to thud inside his chest. For a second his limbs were paralysed, then he back-pedalled in quick recovery. He crouched, listening, his ears cocked to pick up the slightest atom of noise. There was complete silence except for a slight breeze that was blowing. Joe contained the urge to shout out. This silence was more un-nerving than anything he had experienced. Something like a lizard or rat moved overhead and fell on the ground with a thud that startled him and made him jump back in alarm. Struggling to stop the painful beating of his heart, his finger tightened on the trigger.

There was a scratching noise on the wall that made his heart lurch violently. He crouched against the ambulance and waited. Suddenly something like a block hit the ground in front of him and spattered him with sand. In his panic, before he realized it was sand, his hand squeezed the trigger involuntarily and the shot exploded inside the garage with a flash of fire.

When the echo died down the scratching noises continued. Joe could bear it no longer.

"Look Gilt . . . . I know you're there." His words were slow and distinct. "Seems you'll never leave your old tricks. I know you haven't got a gun. If you don't want me to blast out your guts better get away now . . . ."

A stinking decomposing chuck of dead flesh landed on his face and this made him more nervous. "Don't think you can scare me by throwing decomposing flesh at me. I know you're the guy Gilt . . . . . the same old, mean dirty tricks. This time I could open a bloody large hole in your guts if you don't stop these pranks."

Two more chunks hit him in the face.

"Gilt . . . . Gilt . . . . Gilt . . . . Gilt." As he called the name repeatedly in a desperate effort to bolster his sagging confidence and locate Gilt's position, the echo of his voice sounded deep and ominous which scared him more.

"This is your last chance Gilt." He said, trying to instill false confidence in his voice but he couldn't camouflage the quaver in it. "I'll give you ten seconds to get out. After that if you're still here I'll come searching for you. I've got a gun, you haven't. Don't kid yourself you can outsmart me. Your mean tricks wouldn't get you anywhere. Ten seconds ..., ... after that you're living on borrowed time."

Something came whistling past him hitting the wall with a dull thud. He started back and stepped on one·of the dead bodies. With a startled cry he pulled the trigger again and again. Amidst the deafening bangs of the gun he heard Pat screaming hysterically. Involuntarily he glanced briefly at the ambulance. A slight sound beside him made him spin around but he was too late.

A violent blow on the arm sent his gun skittering on the floor. A knife plunged into his arm. With a yelp of pain he twisted aside, lashing out violently with his foot and catching Gilt off guard. They fought violently and fiercely — Puna with the thought that his opponent was wielding a knife. But his blood was ebbing away and with that his strength. A blow staggered him against the ambulance and another made his kness buckle under him. He was vaguely aware of steely fingers closing around his scrawny throat, shutting out the supply of air to his lungs. He put up a weak struggle but it was no use against the sapping weight that held him pinned to the ground. His eardrums were bursting. A chuckle .... somehow maniacal, sounded from afar. The last thing he saw was two glittering eyes in the darkness before the lights in his life went out.

B

Young and Ify came barging into the garage and stopped dead in their tracks as the odour of decomposing matter coupled with the smell of cordite wafted into their nostrils. They had been in each other's arms when the sound of gun shots woke them. They'd only waited to scramble into their clothes. Not being sure whether it was the police or not, they had checked up Gilt but he wasn't in the room. Neither was Puna. Nor even their captive Pat. Feeling apprehensive they had come barging out of the house and into the garage.

"Who's there?" Bill asked, fumbling for the light switch as Ify clung to his arm.

A movement nearby almost startled him. "Who's there?" He repeated, moving a step back.

"Watch it." Jimoh's clear voice came distinctly to them. "I've got a gun. I could use it."

Just then Bill's hand located the light switch and he thumbed it on. For an instant the light hit him then as his eyes became used to it, sweat broke out on his forehead. For facing them was Gilt, his legs slightly apart and a snub-nosed gun in his hand. There was a satiated stupid expression on his face. Looking at his unnaturally bright eyes and the slightly mangled corpse that had been Joe Puna sent a cold shudder down Bill's young spine. Ify's hand had gone into her mouth in stupefied horror.

Noticing their scared reactions Jimoh grinned stupidly at them.

"That's a lesson to anyone who thinks he can outsmart me. Two of you shouldn't kid yourselves you can succeed where he failed. Joe was miles smarter than two of you put together. Make a false move and I'll drill you full of holes before you know it."

Young's hands, clammy with sweat shook a little. "Look Gilt," he forced himself to meet the eunuch's eyes, "we need an explanation. What's happened to Joe? We don't know nothing."

"Joe tried to outsmart me just as the two of you are thinking now." The eunuch went on glibly for unknown to the others the last chord of sanity in his revenge-crazy mind had snapped. "So you two thought you could outsmart me as well eh?" There was a sneer in his voice, then his eyes hardened.

"Raise your hands fast!"

"Look Gilt . . . ."

"I said, raise your hands!" The eunuch snarled, standing flat-footed, his eyes glittering and his finger tightening on the trigger.

The two slowly raised their hands.

"To the wall!"

Again they obeyed.

The eunuch chuckled maniacally the stupid expression still on his face. He began toying with the gun.

Meanwhile the two police vehicles were approaching Woods Avenue. Ogunbor had heard the firing with the rest of the crew and he'd ordered the driver to accelerate. Now racing at a dangerous seventy miles an hour, their car turned into Woods Avenue.

"Slow down a bit." Ogunbor ordered as the tires skidded dangerously.

The car slowed down gradually and slid to a stop after some further metres. Twenty metres ahead was a sign post that had 4B Woods Avenue written on it. The second car stopped behind them and the occupants scrambled out. It took Ogunbor time to bring out his bulk. Surveying the surroundings the Chief of Police instinctively knew that this was the robbers' hideout. The whole place was silent and eerie, the apartment the only one on this Avenue, as far as the eye could see. He could have sworn there wasn't anyone inside the house if not for those gun-shots.

"We'll surround the house." He said to the men. "Baba, take your two lieutenants and confront them. We'll be ready if they try to get rough."

Baba nodded and motioned to his two lieutenants. One of them had a powerful torch with him. On nearing the garage Baba could hear voices and there was a light on. He paused a moment to release the safety catch on his gun and make sure that the sharp-shooters were surrounding the house. Then they drew nearer.

He could hear the voices distinctly. One was saying: "I'm old in this game and I know all the angles. I knew that sooner or later you guys would start getting crazy ideas about a double-cross. I can't say I blame you. With all that money around even a monk would get ideas."

"Look Gilt, I've been with you all these years. When the police were hot on my tracks you were the guy who gave me protection. You saved my skin so why should I turn against you. I swear that none of us was trying to double-cross you."

Baba grinned. So the rogues were beginning to quarrel about the bread. He went a step closer and peeped inside. One of the robbers had a man and a woman cowering against the wall. He could see the ambulance inside the garage, a mutilated body on the floor and two decomposing bodies near the door. The stink of decomposing matter hit him squarely and made him wrinkle his nose in disgust. He couldn't help thinking to himself that this was a cheap round up — only one of the robbers had a gun. Once disarmed, the rest were theirs.

They came out into the open, about two yards from the garage door.

"Freeze!" Baba barked in his hard cop voice, his .45 automatic levelled at Jimoh. "This gun is powerful. It can tear off a guy's head."

The eunuch was crazy! Stark crazy! Without looking he spun around and fired, diving for the light switch as Baba's .45 thundered with violent power. One of Baba's lieutenants took Jimoh's bullet on the hand, dropping his gun and falling to his knees with a yelp of pain. Baba's powerful .45 tore at Ify's chest, jerking her back and forth and killing her instantly. Baba and his remaining lieutenant were already diving to the ground as the light in the garage went out. They dragged out their wounded colleague as the sharpshooters began pounding the garage.

Young caught Ify as she began to fall and held her to him. His heart was heavy as he felt her pulse. A dying pulse. A change came over him instantly. Suddenly he wasn't afraid to die any longer. He wanted to join her for he'd fallen madly in love with her. He felt a little lightheaded and reckless.

"See what you've caused, you lousy, perverted eunuch." He rasped in a cold unafraid voice. "If it hadn't been for you, she wouldn't have gotten killed. All right. I'm going to revenge her. I'm going to kill you."

With lightning speed he darted outside and grabbed the fallen rifle of the wounded policeman just as a searchlight illuminated him. The rifle in his hand barked out a desperate message of death. The cop with the searchlight was thrown backwards and he lay moaning on the ground in a gathering pool of his own blood.

Young yelped triumphantly and sprinted for the door of the garage. A rifle boomed in the darkness. The bullet smashed into his hip bone forcing him down on one knee. His yelp of pain was lost in the muffle as a second rifle banged. The slug struck his spine making him to bend double. With a sudden defiant revival he squeezed off two aimless shots before another slug tore into the biceps of his arms. The rifle slipped out of his fingers and he fell face downwards on the ground. Moaning with pain his fingers clawed desperately for his fallen gun. He was still clawing when six guns spat fire simultaneously. His body jerked once and lay still.

Jimoh who had been observing warily as Young was riddled to death, lay on the bonnet of the ambulance. His cunning mind was already racing for a way out. Next moment he was off the bonnet like a coiled spring. He sparked off a shot with the .38 Positive to keep the police occupied, then jerked open the door and jumped into the driver's seat. Grabbing Pat's head savagely he drew her body towards him and then dropped her head on his laps. She had fainted inside the ambulance during his death-battle with Puna and now looking at her pale lovely face the eunuch had a hunch that she was his sure ticket out of this death trap. Putting the gun to her head his voice boomed inside the garage.

"Listen to me, you lousy numbskulls." He said, speaking distinctly above the lull in the fighting. There was a moment of suspense among the cops raiding the garage. He continued. All the cops in this city are lousy numb skulls. You guys shouldn't think you could have latched unto me if my gang had played by my rules. I have a nice lady here — my captive. If any of you makes a false move towards me I would blow her brains out. Get me? I've a gun on her skull right now and I'm getting away in this ambulance. If you want to pick her brains from my laps, then make a false move. I'm not tired of killing yet."

Lying in a patch of grass across the road, his pistol trained on the garage door, Ogunbor discovered he was sweating. He flicked away the sweat on his fat face with his fingers and wiped them on the seat of his pants.

"Look mister whatever your name is," Ogunbor began, trying to stall and gain time to think. At the moment he wasn't sure of what to do. He knew that the threat he'd just heard was genuine — the guy wouldn't hesitate to kill the captive if he had any there. "Don't try to be a dead hero. Come out with your hands held high in the air. You wouldn't get hurt. I'd better advise you not to play cagey as that would get you nowhere."

"A false move and you'll be picking her brains up." Jimoh chuckled. "Don't try to stop me. I'm driving out now."

He tried to start the vehicle and was startled to discover that the key wasn't there.He'd forgotten that Puna had the key. Moving stealthily in the dark, he opened the door and acted with lightning speed. Grabbing Puna's dead body, he dragged it back to the ambulance, climbed back onto the driver's seat and began going through the pockets. Finding the key, he shoved the body away from the door and banged it. Then he plugged the key in, started the ambulance and put the gear in reverse. He moved the mini-bus out of the garage, his left hand maneuvering the seering and his right hand holding the gun against the captive's temple. Once clear of the garage, he paused to wipe the sweat on his face, his heart hammering.

"Don't try to follow me." His voice boomed out again with an almost hypnotic spell. "I wouldn't warn you guys again. A false move and her brains will be scattered on my laps."

He changed the gear and sent the ambulance crawling forward. The tires were deflated, the wheels scraping the surface of the road as the ambulance moved past the bewildered policemen. Once past the squad cars, he dropped the gun on the seat beside him and trod on the gas. The mini-bus surged forward, bouncing from side to side while the wheels rattled ceaselessly.

As the vehicle disappeared from view,Ogunbor seemed to snap out of his reverie.

"What are you guys waiting for?" He snapped. "Get after him! He musn't get away with the money. Baba, take some men and go after him! He must be stopped!"

Baba motioned to two of the men as another flashlight flickered on. He sprinted down the road, closely followed by the men. A minute later they were speeding back the way they'd come, the headlamps of the car lighting up the road ahead with stabbing rays.

As the car took the corner, he switched off the headlights. Some two hundred yards ahead were the disappearing tail lights of the ambulance. The ambulance turned into a dirt road. Seconds later, the police car followed suit.

As the ambulance began bumping over the pot-holes that graced the untarred dirt road, Baba brought the police car to a hurried halt.

"Get after him on foot! Quick! He musn't escape. That's the chief's order."

The two policemen scrambled out and began sprinting after the slow-moving ambulance — now hundred yards away and chug-bumping over the thousands of pot-holes in the road. Thirty seconds later Baba was sprinting in their wake, his .45 automatic ready for battle.

Presently the two policemen caught up with the ambulance.

Jimoh suddenly stiffened as something tinkled near him. Glancing beside him he froze.

A Thompson sub-machine gun mounted on the open window of the moving ambulance was staring at him and the owner running along side the ambulance to keep pace.

"Stop that ambulance." A young cop-voice panted. "And don't be a smart fool. It wouldn't get you anywhere. There are two guns on you."

Jimoh shifted on the seat to glance at the other window. Another Thompson-sub was staring at him, its cold gaping muzzle uncaring.

In that instant of stark reality, Jimoh's razor-sharp brain raced. If he surrendered there was no hope. It would be the firing squad and a mob of jeering, booing faces. He couldn't hope to beat the death rap. No jury would fail to condemn him. And no Court of Appeal would alter the death penalty. Whereas if he tried, there was still a chance of survival.

He jammed his foot on the break-pedal and as the vehicle began to slow down, his right hand hovered over the ignition key. Glancing casually at the door handle, he suddenly bent low under the direct range of the guns. In the same lightning move, his left hand jerked open the door, shoving it into the face of the young cop and his right hand grabbing his own gun in the process.

He dived through the open door as the Thompson on his right window belched flame. A slug tore into his left bicep, tearing through tendons and bone. The searing pain hit him as he landed on the fallen cop. Through reflex borne out of rage and pain coupled with the animal instinct for survival the .38 in his hand thundered at close range. The cops left eye disappeared to be replaced by a yawning crimson cavity.

With the pain in his arm acute, Jimoh grabbed the guy's sub and zig-zagging into the bush threw himself behind a shrub as Baba came tearing up to the dying cop.

Peering at the bloody cavity where his young lieutenant's eye had been, Baba felt his guts contract into a tight knot. As he made to lift the young man whose life was ebbing fast, something clicked in his brain.

'See what you've caused you lousy, perverted eunuch.'

One of the robbers had said this before he was killed. And he'd meant the guy they were now after. So the guy they were now after was a eunuch. A eunuch!

'If you come across a eunuch better be careful how you handle him . . . . . any trouble and there's a eunuch, get away as fast as possible.' That was what the fortune-teller had said to him on that day. Maybe there was something in that warning. Could be the fortune-teller knew what he was saying. He'd be better alive without ten thousand bread as a reward than bullet holes over his dead body and a hero's funeral.

"Get after him." Baba said to the other policeman who had sidled over to his side. "He's behind one of those shrubs. Better be careful while you go about it. Though injured, he's still a dangerous customer." He paused then added. "I'm coming to help you. Let me just remove our friend from the line of fire."

As the young eager policeman dashed off into the bush, Baba lifted the dying one onto his shoulders and carried him to the back of the ambulance. Opening the door he laid the youngster inside. Immediately the youngster's good eye fluttered slightly open. His face was contorted with pain. His lips were moving in a futile bid to speak. Then his head rolled sideways and he died.

Baba got up slowly for he'd been kneeling beside the dead cop.

It was then his eyes focused on the crates of money inside the ambulance. His heart lurched and then began to bang unevenly. Moving towards one of the crates, he opened it slowly with shaking hands. The sight of the neatly packed bills made him gasp involuntarily. His mouth had suddenly gone dry.

Carry it! A voice was telling him. You can hide it in the bush where no one will see it. With this sort of money you can retire conveniently from the Force.

Suddenly Baba's dishonest mind was made up. He was going to hide the crate.

Crouching so that his head wouldn't have to hit the roof of the ambulance, he advanced to the glass partition separating the back of the vehicle from the front and peered through it. A lady was sprawled back on the seat, obviously in a coma.

Now was the time, he told himself.

Above the din and rattle of automatic fire, he carried the crate out of the ambulance. His chest heaving, he glanced up to make sure no one was watching him. Then carrying the crate, he began moving away.

He felt a hot scorching pain shoot up from his thigh. In panic he dropped the crate. The crate hit the ground and split open, wads of nice cool naira rolling out. Valuing his life more than the money, Baba hit the dust as a Thompson-sub rattled somewhere behind a shrub. Slugs whistled and whined around him. One pierced through his police uniform.

Gritting his teeth he crawled into the bush, his heart heaving as more flame continued to belch from the gun. He waited first for his eyes to adjust well to the diluted darkness then he peered around, trying to locate his lieutenant.

Finally he saw him, lying behind a small tree and spraying the bush ahead with slugs. Baba crawled in beside him, then examined the wound on his thigh. It wasn't much. Just more than a graze but he was bleeding and his trousers were already soaked.

"Keep on firing at him." Baba told the young policeman who was glancing anxiously at his leg. "Just a graze. I'm going after him. Don't try to bring your head out. That guy's probably a sharpshooter. Eku's bought it. I don't want anything to happen to you."

Then he crawled out again into the night.

Jimoh meanwhile released another burst from the sub. He was keeping the gun steady with his left armpit for the hand was almost useless. His face was wracked with pain as he continued firing defiantly, watching his blood flowing away. The shrub afforded much protection against any direct fire.

He paused a moment to examine the wound again. A grimace etched his face as he felt the extent of the wound. The bullet had pierced the bone leaving some pieces hanging out. It was likely he would never use the hand again. If he survived the arm would be amputated. A eunuch and next an amputee. No it wouldn't happen, he told himself. He would fight to the last breath and probably take those two with him. They had stopped his escape bid and so deserved to die. He couldn't imagine how the police had found out their hideout unless they were near when Joe was shooting indiscriminately. It was probably one of his damned gangsters who'd goofed his carefully laid-out plans. Well, his final bite wasn't going to be goofed by any silly punk. He was taking care of it himself. It would be a grand, fitting finale to one of the greatest escapades ever. Posterity would remember him as a robber. Yeah. But they were going to remember him as a robber of class who died in a classy way. In his demented mind's eye he could see a funeral procession with a huge crowd gathered and all the people he'd killed carrying his coffin. The sight! The beauty! The sheer class of it all!

A slug ploughed a furrow on his forehead making him snap out of his mad reverie.

He remembered what he'd said: 'If you want to grow rich, there's no easier road mister.'

Yeah. True. But Furo had been right too: 'No easier road to destruction, mister.'

Suddenly he jerked back to reality. Where was the other cop? Only one was firing. A twig broke near him. He spun around wildly, trying to swing the Tommy gun with his ebbing strength. A .45 thundered at close range. The slug smashed into his ribs.

With a yelp of pain he half rose to his feet. The young cop still behind his tree, loosened a burst from his gun. Jimoh felt the tracers pouring into him. He sank to one knee.

He was dimly aware of Baba's bulk rising near him. Well if I'm dying, why not finish myself? Jimoh thought. In that way no one would have the honour of finishing the robber of class.

His hand moved slowly as he lay on the ground. Then smiling, his face wracked with pain, he put the gun against his temple and pressed the trigger.